The Jewish War

and

The Victory

THE JEWISH WAR

and

THE VICTORY

HENRYK GRYNBERG

NORTHWESTERN UNIVERSITY PRESS

Evanston, Illinois

Northwestern University Press
Evanston, Illinois 60208-4210

Printed in the United States of America

10 9 8 7 6 5 4 3 2 1

ISBN 0-8101-1901-3 (cloth)
ISBN 0-8101-1785-1 (paper)

Library of Congress Cataloging-in-Publication Data

Grynberg, Henryk.
    [Żydowska wojna. English]
    The Jewish war ; and, The victory / Henryk Grynberg ; translated from the Polish by Celina Wieniewska with the author and by Richard Lourie.
    p. cm. — (Jewish lives)
    ISBN 0-8101-1901-3 (cloth : alk. paper) — ISBN 0-8101-1785-1 (pbk. : alk. paper)
    I. Title: Jewish war ; and, The victory. II. Wieniewska, Celina. III. Lourie, Richard, 1940– IV. Grynberg, Henryk. Zwycięstwo. English. V. Title: Victory. VI. Title. VII. Series.

PG7166.R86 Z4513 2001
891.8'5373—dc21

2001030976

The Jewish War was translated from the Polish by Celina Wieniewska with the author. *The Victory* was translated from the Polish by Richard Lourie.

✿

Contents

❖

Author's Note

The Jewish War, my first full-size prose, written and published in Warsaw in 1965, became a subject of controversy because it differed from official prescriptions for depicting the Nazi Occupation and the fate of the Jews. All reviews were held up by the censorship. The book was saved by Jarosław Iwaszkiewicz, the most influential author of the time, who prevailed and, on May 1, 1966, devoted to it his weekly literary column. Among the qualities of the book, he included "thousands of concealments" behind the text. Self-censorship, undoubtedly one of the reasons for those concealments, prompted me also to mix some fictitious elements into this autobiographical story, including some names of persons and places. In this edition most of the fiction has been eliminated.

The sequel, entitled The Victory, I wrote in California in 1968, immediately after becoming a self-exile. It was published in January 1969 by the Institut Littéraire near Paris, the Polish émigré publisher of Witold Gombrowicz and Czesław Miłosz. It had several reprintings in the underground Polish press of the 1980s before its legal publication by the Dominicans' press in Poznań in 1990.

Written as an independent, autonomous book, The Victory contained some repeats of events described in The Jewish War. This edition of two books in one required several adjustments, including elimination of those repetitions. The Victory, second of my five-book cycle on wartime and postwar Polish-Jewish experience, starts where other Holocaust stories usually end: at the liberation. It attempts to describe the fate of the survivors immediately after the catastrophe, presenting the liberation as not an end but a sequel to their suffering. They had to cope with their immeasurable losses in the post-Holocaust reality where fear—particularly fear of being a Jew—had no end. Still defenseless, they depended on the protection of a foreign army and an unpopular regime. Pawns of a cruel political struggle and easy targets in a simmering civil war, they were forced into costly moral compromises with no help or even concern for their posttraumatic stress.

THE JEWISH WAR

*I am puzzled and awed by the price of human life. This is why
I have to tell the story of my father's inescapable destiny and
of the unbelievable resilience of a woman who fought alone,
my mother.*

—H.G., WARSAW, 1965

.

Part I

Father

My father ran to see the squire, bribed the gendarmes, and did all he could. The squire pleaded with the Germans that Father was indispensable on the estate, and, if they really cared about the prompt delivery of all those quotas they demanded, they should allow Father to stay on the estate for as long as possible. So Father continued to run the dairy and helped with the accounts as before, the only difference being that now it was always Father who owed the squire, not the other way around. This arrangement held good for a year.

The squire helped us this way as long as he could. When nothing more could be done, Father loaded part of our bundles on a cart that he had borrowed from the squire—part of them, for he had left most valuable things with the squire and other people for safekeeping— and we set out for the little town in which my mother's family lived and where my paternal grandfather with his family had already been resettled from a neighboring estate. There we made our home in one room of a tenement that belonged to Grandfather. Both Father and Grandfather had to go out every day to break stones on the highway. But things got worse when the Germans started sending people to a camp near Węgrów. It all began with flour and sugar.

A certain quota of flour and sugar had been allotted to the shtetl, and the task of the local Council was to distribute the flour and sugar on rations. But there wasn't enough flour and sugar even for those who had ration coupons. So first come, first served, and those who came later were left with their coupons but no rations. After a while it transpired that those who paid the cash equivalent of a certain number of coupons always arrived in time, and those who had no money came always "too late."

Father had money, so everything was in order, until the Council sold half of the sugar quota in Mińsk Mazowiecki and half the population, defined as "less needy," did not get their ration coupons at all. We found ourselves in that category. Father went to see Nusen, who was chairman of the Council, to clarify the matter. While there, he noticed behind the glass of Nusen's sideboard a whole batch of undistributed ration coupons.

"Why didn't you give me any coupons for sugar?" asked Father.

"Because there is no sugar; they only allotted half the quota."

"So why did they give all those coupons?" said Father, moving nearer to the sideboard.

"Which coupons?" Nusen wondered.

"These!" said Father, reaching for the batch behind the glass.

Nusen rushed at him to get it back, but Father ran out with it into the street. Nusen followed, but Father ran straight to the Polish police, to Laskowski, who was in charge, and handed him the coupons.

This forced Nusen to give Father our coupons and to make sure that we got our rations, and Laskowski told Father that he had acted correctly. But, when the Germans demanded from Nusen an additional quota of men for the camp at Węgrów, he put Father's name on the list.

While Father was in the camp where he dug ditches by the side of the road, we fell ill with typhus. As soon as he heard about it, Father started to look for ways of escape. One day the German supervisor noticed that in some places Father was digging deeply, as he was supposed to, but in other, less visible places, he had barely scratched the surface.

"*Komm hier!*" the German called, and, when Father approached, he struck him with a riding crop that had an iron knob at the end.

"Is this how you dig?" he shouted.

Father returned to his ditch and started digging as deeply as he could as long as the German was looking. But, as soon as the German walked away and a Polish policeman replaced him, Father pressed his hands to his stomach and said that he got diarrhea from fear of the German and needed to go in the bushes. Since the bushes grew all the way to the forest, Father went and did not turn back but hid in the forest, and the following day returned home to us.

Father hired a cart from a peasant, put Mother and me on it, leaving my little brother, Buciek, at Grandpa's. He drove us to the hospital. He did not take us to Mińsk Mazowiecki where they simply let the sick lie unattended until they died but to a real hospital in Węgrów. He did not ride on the cart but walked beside it, helping the horse. At that time he was already sick, too, so, when we arrived in Węgrów, he was laid up with us.

Father was still sick when Mother and I recovered, so we returned from the hospital without him. Then it turned out that our room had been taken by someone else, and Chairman Nusen allotted us a place in the barracks, with the poor people. When Father came home from the hospital, he was very thin and could barely walk but went to see Nusen the same evening.

"How dare you? You allot to some strangers a room in the house that belongs to my father and make my wife and child who have just recovered from typhus live in barracks with beggars!"

"And what are you thinking of?" replied Nusen. "You escape from camp and I have to answer for it? You're lucky not to have been caught. You and your family aren't on the list of residents anymore. How was I to know they would come back from the hospital? Do many people come back from there?"

Nusen had a wife, Frymka, who was older than he, and he always did what she told him to. He also had two pretty and well-nourished children, who both wore white tights and long hair, so that one could not tell which was a girl and which a boy.

"Why did you send me to camp?" Father persisted, though he felt his case was shaky.

"And whom did you expect me to send? I sent everybody who's fit for work. Would you have wanted me to go myself?"

"Why didn't you send those knaves with wooden clubs, those criminals who are serving here as your police?"

"Don't you meddle with my official duties!" shouted Nusen, and banged the table with his fist.

At that moment Father noticed that, under the table, covered with a long cloth, lay a neatly severed head of a black heifer. For fat Nusen was a butcher who had his own butcher's shop before the war and later ran illegal slaughter with other butchers and some cattle traders. This was well known.

"I won't meddle with your duties if you allot me and my family a decent place to live," said Father calmly.

"And if I don't?"

"If you don't. . . ." Father bent down and pulled the severed head from under the table by its ears. In addition he gave Nusen some amount of cash, and we could live like human beings again, although our names did not appear on the list of the shtetl's residents.

But this did not last long either. Toward the end of the summer, the men rushed out more frequently than ever to read official announcements posted in the market square and returned home with anxious eyes. During muffled conversations at home, plates slipped out of women's hands. At the gray hour of dusk, the women wrapped themselves in large woolen shawls under which they had hidden little bundles and sneaked out to the houses of their fair-haired neighbors.

In the autumn, squeaking carts borrowed from peasants and loaded with pillows and eiderdown set off in the direction of Stanisławów. Once again we rode on the cart, while Father walked alongside in his high boots, occasionally pushing the cart with his shoulders, which were always slightly uplifted as if bearing an invisible burden. His brows were frowning and seemed even thicker because of it, the blue shave shadows on his cheeks reached almost to his eyes, and in the September sun his thick, stiff, and unruly hair glistened with purple.

It is hard to tell how much Father knew and how much he only guessed. In any case, he had never trusted anybody very much, least of all the Germans, and had faith only in himself. Therefore, in Stanisławów, which, as it transpired, was not to be our destination but only another stage in our destiny, on that night when it was learned that the next morning entire families were to turn up with hand luggage no bigger than they could carry, Father decided that we wouldn't turn up anywhere anymore. Whoever was able to do so would run immediately to the countryside, and whoever, like grandparents, was unable to run would go into hiding with Gentile friends to sneak out into the country later under cover of night, and, in the country, we would somehow manage. For we were country folk and we knew that, no matter what, one does not perish so quickly in the country as in a town.

We went to bed without undressing, on the contrary, putting on as many clothes as we could. Mother woke me up so early that I felt as if I had only just closed my eyes. The windows were covered over with blankets, and candles were lit as if it were the Sabbath. Mother lifted me from bed because I was unable to get up by myself. She cried as she put my shoes on. Father was busy tying small bundles. Buciek, wrapped in a blue blanket, was still asleep. He could not run either. He was to be left for the time being with people who had many children of their own. He was only eighteen months old and they could say he was their child. But at the last moment Mother changed her mind and did not hand Buciek over to the woman who came for him, and all four of us sneaked out of the house.

Day was beginning to break when we were running along a gray path toward the fields. From all over the place one could hear stamping, knocking, even shots. The shots became more frequent while we were crossing the field. Mother ran with Buciek in her arms, cradled in a big woolen shawl that she had tied around her, and Father was carrying me on his shoulders. Then Mother stopped, and so did Father; now he carried Buciek, and I ran next to him holding his hand. Then Mother stopped again and, breathing heavily, took Buciek from Father, and Father again took me on his shoulders. But Mother turned back with Buciek in her arms, and Father and I reached the countryside without her.

The next time I saw Mother she was sitting in the middle of a room in Głęboczyca, at a peasant's where we had found shelter. She was wearing the same big woolen shawl, but Buciek was not cradled in it now. She was sitting on a stool, in the middle of the room, and smiled when Father brought me in.

"Where is Buciek?" I asked at once.

"He's not here," she replied.

"Where is he then?"

"He's not here."

"Don't worry your mother," said our hostess. "You can see she's tired. If you keep pestering her, she'll go away and not come back at all. You'd better go out and play in the yard."

"But I want to know where Buciek is!" I cried.

Life was good in the country. The country meant an open space, not meeting people one did not want to meet, and only seeing those who were waiting for us in secluded cottages, who gave us food, allowed us to stay the night, knew us. When a stranger had been spotted, we locked ourselves in a spare room where there was rarely anything except a bed—one but big enough that we could all sleep in it—and the door to such room was usually camouflaged on the other side by a large wardrobe.

One day, while we were still in Głęboczyca, Aunt Itka appeared at the farm. Then we learned—not from Aunt Itka but from the farmer who did not tell her that we were there—that Grandfather and Grandmother did not want to hide and had gone to the train. They said they were too old and felt it was undignified for them to wander around homeless and hide with strangers. Grandfather was a Talmudist, known as a man who would not talk to just anybody. Being a Talmudist was not a profession, one did not make any money out of it; therefore, he had little need for people. A Talmudist, Mother explained to me, is a man who wishes to be wise. He had quarreled with Father, not because Father had started his independent life by shaving his cheeks and getting into business with a squire of his own but because he married a girl who was the best looking but also one of the poorest and who, as everybody around said, did not really want to marry him. Neither Grandfather nor anybody else of his family came to the wedding, and he did not set foot in our house until I was born. Grandfather was not interested in other people and their affairs. On the very occasions when he consented to see someone, he offered good advice, brief and very wise, but of a kind that mostly could not be accepted. In Stanisławów, when Father had said that we wouldn't let ourselves be taken anywhere else and had arranged a hiding place for them, Grandfather did not comment, and everybody was convinced that he had agreed. But he went to the train, along with Grandmother and my slightly retarded Uncle Meir and Aunt Rivka, who could have escaped as Itka did but did not want to leave their old parents and poor brother. I don't believe Grandfather had any illusions about the destination of that train. But he also knew what lay in store for those who would escape. He knew everything about human beings, or at least everything that was important, for he had never been interested in their small everyday affairs. He also knew that the human world existed on the basis of a certain covenant whereby certain conditions have been established, and if we ever break them . . . so he went to the train to die voluntarily like a human being. He did not tell us anything, he was too wise for that. Perhaps he was afraid to tell. He wanted us to run away just in case. He was wise.

Our peasant also learned from Itka that Nusen and his wife were in the vicinity and that they had escaped from the train without their lovely children. When Mother heard this, her face began to tremble and she buried it in a pillow, but her shoulders and her back continued to shake.

She had wanted to save Buciek. She had wanted to go into hiding with him but was told that this wouldn't do because Buciek might start talking or crying. Therefore, the peasants hid her alone, and took Buciek to the cottage. Buciek was lovely, with large blue eyes. He seldom cried but liked to make noise when playing. He liked to imitate an airplane.

Mother heard them coming. She was hiding in the loft in the hay, next to the stairs, and could hear everything.

"Whose child is this?" they asked.

"Ours."

"Come on, too good looking to be yours," said one of them.

"And circumcised at that," said the other.

Buciek did not cry. He didn't seem to be afraid. He only looked at them with those large blue eyes, making them laugh. They showed him to each other while taking him away: "What a lovely child." They did not do any harm to the hostess because they were in such a good mood. Mother could not conceal a certain pride when she told us about it.

"Maybe one of them has kept him," she said. "Maybe they didn't do him any harm?"

We remained at Głęboczyca until the middle of the autumn. We might have stayed longer, but a Commission showed up in the vicinity. At first the farmer wanted us to hide in the barn where Aunt Itka had been hidden, but Father said it was not a good idea for everybody to be in the same place. Besides, a barn was not a good hiding place, he said, and it would be better if the farmer told Itka to flee while she could, as she was alone, and it was easier for her to get away.

But Itka was afraid to get out and remained in the barn, while we hid in straw on the loft over the cowshed. The cows were making a noise below us, which made us feel better and made it not so easy to hear us up there.

Through the chinks in the thatch we saw a yellow wagonette come to a stop in the yard and some of the people enter the cottage, while others went into the outbuildings and the barn where Aunt Itka was hidden. They spent some time there, and then reappeared leading her out. She had bits of straw in her long, black plait and was red in the face. She did not speak, only looked around at everybody who was out in the yard. We saw her walking across the yard, ignorant of the fact that we were so near and that we were looking at her all the time. She would never know. Later we stopped gazing out and hid our heads in the straw because we heard the door of the cowshed where we were hiding fling open and the men walking up and down. They did not manage to get up to us because the shed was full of fresh cows' dung and there was no ladder for climbing up to the loft, or maybe it was because the cows started a terrible row and did not stop until the men left. The same evening we left Głęboczyca walking through the forest.

We walked through the forest very often. The forest was damp, smelling of autumn and mist. There were no paths in it, and only Father knew where to go. The forest screened us, but it also screened everything that was in front of us and around us, and this is why we could not feel safe in the forest. For instance, we could be coming from one direction and a forester from another. The forest belonged to him: the trees, the berries, the mushrooms, the meat and skins of animals, and money, of which there was more in the forest at that time than at any other. A forester neither sows nor reaps; he just slings his shotgun on his shoulder and goes into his forest. . . . The forester knew all the places where one could walk, and all the deer and hares would come straight up to him, then stop still or sit up.

"What do you think you are doing?" asked the forester. "Walking about? In the daytime?"

"Well, yes . . . to get some fresh air."

"And with a child? Won't he catch cold?"

"Not likely, sir, . . . the child is used to it. . . ."

"Then it's all right," said the forester slowly. "Quite all right," he repeated, looking at me while I tried to hide by pushing my head against Mother's belly.

Father's hands began to shake and couldn't find his pocket.

"Eh, no need for that, don't look for anything," the forester said gently. "I am not a greedy man. I don't covet what is not mine."

Father's hands stopped still, though they continued to shake.

"Mr. Forester is a kind man," Mother said and tried to smile but her face began to quiver, so she stopped. "We are only passing through, Mr. Forester. We shall pass and continue on our way."

"Yes," said the forester slowly. "I am not a greedy man. What God sends my way is good enough."

Father looked at Mother and saw anxiety in her eyes, so he moved his hand to his coat again.

"I don't need anything," continued the forester, and Father's hand stopped still again. "If a man can save his skin these days, he's rich enough. . . ."

"It's true," answered Father, completely confused.

"How right you are!" Mother eagerly chimed in.

"Who cares today about money or gold? Everybody wants to save his skin."

"So maybe we'll be on our way, Mr. Forester?" asked Father uncertainly.

"I said, everybody wants to save his skin," continued the forester, pretending not to have heard Father. "A man must do now what he is ordered to do. . . ." He sighed. "Such rotten times!"

"But we only, Mr. Forester . . ." Father's hand groped around his coat and eventually found his breast pocket. "We are only passing. . . ."

"Only because it's on our way," added Mother.

"With a child?" The forester smiled sourly.

Father's hands were busily moving from one pocket to another, taking something out and handing it over.

"Please take this, Mr. Forester, please!"

"We'd be so pleased, really, if you would take it."

"Just in case, God forbid, any damage in the forest."

"Exactly. One doesn't look, sometimes unwittingly, one doesn't notice."

"And do you know what happens to a forester, if he doesn't notice?"

"We know, we understand and wouldn't like, God forbid, any un-
pleasantness for you, Mr. Forester, so we shall go at once, all right?"

"And no one will see us here, really. We shall go at once, we won't
stay in this forest, we promise."

"Yes, let's go, let's not waste time. Come, child, say goodbye to the
gentleman and let's go."

"But I can't, my dears," said the forester, shaking the hand in which
Father had put various things for him. "God be my witness, I
can't . . ."

"But we beg you, for your children's sake! Please take all this and
we shall go at once."

"I would like to let you go, God be my witness I would, but the
police post . . . just two kilometers from here. . . ."

"That's nothing, no one will notice. And this, too, please take it,"
said Mother, pulling a ring from her finger. "It's a real stone."

"Ah, the risks a man must take." The forester sighed. "But what
can one do; one must be human. Well, all right then, stop crying,
woman. To tell you the truth, it's because I am sorry for the child,
otherwise . . . show yourself, little boy!"

"No, no, Mummy, no!" I cried, not letting go of Mother's skirt.

"And mind, don't you step here ever again!" shouted the forester from a distance. "Because next time even God Almighty won't
help you."

We hid in the forest until dusk. We sat under the branches of coni-
fers, resting against a trunk where it was dry and quiet. The branches,
growing low, hung down to the ground making a thick shady um-
brella. Only the dry needles shed by the trees plaited in one's hair and
prickled after falling behind one's collar.

When it got dark, Father took leave of us and Mother pulled me
nearer to her and ordered me to sit even more quietly. We looked in
the direction where the branches crackled at first and then swayed up
and down after Father had gone.

We stayed behind alone and never knew when Father would come
back. When? We didn't know if he would come back at all. It depended on so many things. He might get caught, meet someone he
ought not to meet, or just have to hide and wait until late at night.
And we had to sit still and wait for him and not move anywhere so
that he could find us again. And what if they had already got him

and were now looking for us in the forest? Does the rustling and crackling of branches mean that it is Father returning? Sometimes a dried-up twig that has been hanging somewhere between the sky and the earth, no one knows why and what for, suddenly and inexplicably falls down with a dry crack behind one's back. At moments like that our hunger would vanish, and our only desire was that Father should return without delay, that he should bring neither milk nor cold soup, just come back and never leave us again.

And after a time Father always returned bringing a pot full of thick soup, made still thicker by the cold and pine needles that had fallen into it on the way when he was sneaking with it through the dense young trees. The needles continued to drop in while we were eating the soup, so, although very hungry, we had to eat slowly and carefully, avoiding the prickly needles as if it were not soup but fish with fine bones.

And when night fell, we moved on to a barn usually for a night and a day until the following night, sometimes for two days, before walking several kilometers during the night that followed. It was safer, both for us and for the people who gave us shelter, and it was really difficult to track us. At nighttime, when we walked, Father and Mother held me by my hands, Father on one side, Mother on the other. Sometimes they allowed me to sit down for a moment. And, when it was necessary to hurry, Father sat me on his shoulders. As soon as he did so I fell asleep.

We might have wandered in this fashion until late autumn, but this would have become impossible in winter. Therefore, Father was doing everything he could to find a shelter for us before the snows and frosts came. He managed to arrange it with Śliwa, whose farm was situated some distance from the hamlet. Once again we slept in a bed and did not have to be parted from Father every day.

At first at Śliwa's they tried to keep me together with their children, so that I could play and run about in the yard with them. It was thought to be even safer this way. But I had forgotten how to play with children and had no desire to run about, so the disappointed children began to poke me in the ribs and sometimes to smack me harder. I took it all in silence, thinking that it was to be like that, until one day a farmhand dropped in at Śliwa's and started to stare at me while I was sitting on a bench against the wall.

"Whose is he?" he asked. "He can't be yours?"

"No, he was sent by our relatives in town, to fatten him up. You know how things are in town now, hunger and cold. . . ."

"But why is he so quiet?"

"Oh well, a bit underfed, and maybe shy."

"But he looks at one so strangely. . . . He must be a Jewish child."

So afterward I was taken to the other room, which was cold and had boarded-up windows and where Father and Mother were hiding. It was the "best" room, never used during the winter except for a wedding, but no wedding was expected. In the evening Śliwa's wife entered with a pungent-smelling acetylene lamp, and the smell of carbide mingled with the smell of steaming potatoes that she put before us in an iron pot. We also had, just in case, a hideout behind the wardrobe, in a false wall, or rather between two walls, so, in the event of danger, we hid there. We could stand up there or sit down but not lie down. Once we spent a whole day there unable to relieve ourselves. That was the worst. Besides, there was another snag about the hideout: one could enter it only from the front room. This is why, when the village headman came, we couldn't use it.

The headman came after dark. Had he come in the daytime, we would have seen him coming and would have had time to hide. During the day somebody always kept an eye on the road, and the Germans never showed at night. The headman came by night because he knew when to come. He had a word with the farmhand, the one who said of me "He must be a Jewish child." The headman had invited him to his house, they had a few drinks, and then they grabbed two clubs and went to Śliwa's.

Chance had it that on that very night Słoń was also on his way to Śliwa's. He was a friend of my Uncle Aron. He was blond, an albino, and could easily pass as a Gentile. He did not know that we were hiding in Śliwa's best room, but he was worried when he saw the headman and the farmhand, both with large knotty clubs, on the way to Śliwa's farm. Słoń, who had also had a drink that night, hailed them, bade them good evening, and asked where they were going.

"To Śliwa's," they answered.

"To Śliwa's? What for?"

"To look for Jews."

"For Jews?"

"Yes, for Jews."

"Well, then I'm coming with you," said Słoń.

They arrived and Słoń at once said very loudly, "Praise be the Lord, Mr. Śliwa, we have come here to look for Jews!"

Śliwa looked at Słoń, not knowing which of them had gone mad, he or Słoń.

"We heard that you are hiding Jews here," said the headman.

"You must be drunk, Mr. Headman, to joke like that," smiled Śliwa's wife. "We are supposed to hide Jews?"

But the headman wasn't joking and said that he would like to look.

"Please yourself," said Śliwa's wife, although her throat was dry and she felt her knees shaking. But the fact that Słoń was there gave her some courage, so, handing to the headman the key to our room, she turned with the other hand a revolving wooden hasp fastened with one nail over the door and barely visible from behind the wardrobe.

The headman turned the key, but the door did not open. He turned it again, but it still held firm. Then again he tried it once or twice—to no avail.

"There is somebody inside holding the door," said the headman.

"There is no one there," contradicted Śliwa.

"Who can possibly hold when there is no one there?" asked his wife with a naive smile.

"And I tell you there is somebody in there!" insisted the headman, putting his ear against the door.

"You are imagining it, Mr. Headman, I can't hear anything," said Śliwa's wife, also putting her ear to the door.

"Nor can I," said Słoń, having done the same.

"I clearly hear some grating," said the farmhand, having listened in turn.

"Maybe it is mice or a cat," said Śliwa tentatively.

"I would think mice," said Słoń, exchanging a look with Śliwa.

"But there must be someone holding the door from the inside; otherwise, it would have opened," reasoned the headman.

"No one is holding it, Mr. Headman, you must be too tipsy and can't even open the door."

Eventually the headman noticed the hasp, turned it, and opened the door. He threw it wide open and stood there with the farmhand at his side, while Śliwa and Słoń kept closely behind them and Śliwa's wife was leaning against the wall. But the best room was, in fact, empty at the time, a piercing wind was blowing from one of the windows, and the planks, pushed out by Father with his bare hands, were still swinging.

Meanwhile, we were rushing through fluffy white fields, leaving deep dark footmarks behind. We had already gone quite far when the moon appeared over the white heads of trees and lightened that silvery world of winter tales. White puffs steamed from our mouths, and our legs were sinking ever deeper into the snow. I had no strength left to pull my legs out—they were too short for this depth of snow—so Father and Mother pulled me out of the snow by my arms. Soon my arms began to ache, and I cried, asking them to slow down because I could not walk any farther. But they did not slow down, and Father would not let me cry lest anyone hear me. So I stopped crying and only asked them to halt for a rest. But they said we could not halt because the others might catch up with us, and besides we must get somewhere before the end of the night. So I begged them to stop only for a moment. But they wouldn't, even for a moment, because if we stopped, I might fall asleep. That would be all right, I said, because I wanted to sleep, and I let go of Father's hand and slipped into the snow. But I snuggled to its softness only for a short moment because Father pulled me out, shouting something straight into my ear, and dragged me by my arms. He threatened that, if I didn't try to walk, they would leave me and walk away. But I was not afraid and said that it would be quite all right because I didn't want to go anywhere anymore. Then Mother began to cry and begged me to walk a little longer because neither she nor Father had the strength to pull me. So I told them to leave me just for a moment, so I could rest, and as soon as I had rested I would follow them and catch up with them, could they please leave me and go. . . . I did not hear what they replied because my legs got completely entangled in the snow. I could not see anything because my eyes were glazed over with tears, so I closed them, and at once started to dream of large, soft bedding on which I was not allowed to lie down because someone was running after me, chasing me and shouting at me. So I had to run through this white bedding that was giving way under me, and I was sinking in it unable to pull out my feet. I felt a great pain in my knees and in my arms, which I was stretching out in front of me, and the enormous weight of frustrated effort one feels in a dream.

I was awakened by the barking of a dog and the well-known smell of cowshed and stable. I was sitting propped against Mother's knees under a leafless wintry bush. Father, as was usual in such situations, was sneaking up toward the buildings, and Mother and I waited for the dog to stop barking before we followed. The door of the cowshed squeaked softly, and Father showed Mother a ladder. She was to get on first. When Mother got to the top, we could hear the rustle of the straw or hay in which she was making a shakedown, and then Father lifted me up and Mother got hold of me with her arms reaching down from the darkness. This looked uncanny, but I knew that the out-stretched arms were my mother's.

The cows had woken up and became anxious, but Father calmed them, calling them by their names. As it happened, he knew them well, and they knew him, too. For these were his own cows standing in their old place in the squire's shed, and we were back again, almost at home. Father pushed a large bottle in my mouth. It was full of warm milk straight from the cow, and I was falling asleep drinking it. He woke me and tilted the bottle even more until I couldn't drink fast enough and choked on it and, falling asleep again, felt its pleasant warmth streaming down my cheeks and my neck and into my ears.

We were back at home again, and we were milking our own cows. All day long we could hear around the buildings the voices of our former neighbors, although none of them knew that we were so near, as if we were living among them again. As if we were ghosts who had come to our old haunts to look at the places and people among whom we had lived, while they were unaware that someone invisible was around.

It was only the next night that Father knocked at the squire's windows and woke him and his wife, apologizing for having done so and asking their permission to stay in the cowshed. This was granted, but the squire told us to hide in the granary during the day. The squire's wife gave Father bread and milk, a warm shawl for Mother, and a scarf and a pair of gloves for me.

We lay in the cowshed or between the sacks in the granary and listened to the voices of farmhands, to the sounds of cows and horses, the squeaking of the winch and the clanking of buckets at the well, and it seemed as if nothing had happened in the meantime. Our house stood in the same place as before, the cows mooed, people were getting water by the old squeaking winch; both days and nights were the same as before. So perhaps nothing much has happened, we thought, and this plucked up our courage.

While Mother and I waited in the cowshed or in the granary, Father went to look for Słoń. He knew from Śliwa were he was hiding, and with Słoń's help he found the dugout of my mother's family in a forest at Bidula.

When we got there, Grandma gave a party for us. A campfire was lit in front of the dugout. She cooked noodles from the flour that Father had brought, and we ate them with milk. Whoever felt like it sat by the fire; others walked up and down among the trees to straighten their legs and to breathe the fresh air. Grandpa and Grandma looked sickly. Aunts had their hair cut short like men and were wearing men's jackets. Their young brother, whom I never addressed as an uncle because he was only thirteen, was very pale and complained that he was going blind. Before dawn the fire was carefully extinguished and covered up, and we lay down in a row at the bottom of the dugout.

The dugout was deep, solidly reinforced with pales and lined up with twigs and straw. It was neither cold nor damp, and there was enough room for everybody, but it was dark there. In the daytime light came in only through the thin chinks made for air, and at night from the discreet campfire or from the moon—as if the world were plunged into perpetual night. The most fortunate were those of us who were able to sleep during the day and not feel the biting of the lice. By night we went out to relieve ourselves, took off our shirts, and shook the lice off into the fire. Mother cried because she could not pick the lice from my hair quickly enough. She despaired that they were so big. Father tried to comfort her, saying that, if we only endured the winter, he'd find a better place again, but for the time being we should not move because it was easy to track us down in the snow and we might freeze to death on the way.

Słoń's group was hiding in the area. It consisted of the brothers Brzozak—Big Nutek, Biumek, Manes, and Abel—my uncle Aron, and some other men who were single or failed to save their families.

Men alone, they held out in the forest longer than anybody else. Also my father joined them later on, when he was alone. Uncle Aron had been married to my eldest aunt, Feyga, sister of poor Aunt Itka who was taken by the police from the barn at Głęboczyca. Aron courted my mother at one time, but my father beat him to it. Aron and Feyga had lived in Rembertów where he helped Nutek and Biumek to get and deliver cattle for illegal slaughter. After the Jews in Rembertów had been shut in behind barbed wire, Nutek, Biumek, and Aron would bribe the guards and get out at night to return after a couple of nights bringing with them cows with gags in their mouths. One could say that they were the principal providers of the ghetto and that, if this was what the war was about, they would manage to survive. But, once when they left and stayed away for two nights, the Rembertów ghetto disappeared, and they were left alone. Nutek's wife, Esterka, who managed to hide, bleached her hair and went to Warsaw where someone provided her with Aryan papers. The younger of the Brzozaks, Abel, saved himself and Biumek's daughter. They had walked to the train along with Biumek's wife, who was carrying her younger girl in her arms. In Falenica, as they were about to get on the train, Abel ran between loose cars at the siding, pulling his little niece by the hand. They rushed into a backyard garden. It was summer, but they were wearing their best winter clothes, of which they had put on as many as they could. In the garden stood two old women who only needed to glance at them to understand who they were. The women hid them in a cellar. The roundup, with police dogs, lasted the whole day, but the old women poured water on the garden path and sprinkled it with yellow sand as if it were Easter. The girl was later hidden with the Śliwas and afterward, when we were staying there, with the Sadowskis.

Abel perished six months later, together with Manes, when they went to see Podorewski. Biumek and Słoń advised them not to go there, but it was winter and they were hungry. Podorewski was the owner of Piwki, an estate with the best soil in the area. He was the richest and the best-educated squire we knew, with a degree in philosophy, and the Brzozaks had traded with him in the past.

They did not go to him to get money or the valuables that they had left with him. They only wanted some flour, groats, potatoes, and lard. Podorewski let them in and agreed to give them everything they

needed, if they hid for the time being in the cellar so no one would
see them while everything was getting ready. As soon as they descended into a deep black hole, Podorewski shut the trapdoor over
their heads, pulled a heavy chest on the top, and sat down on it, waiting
for the Germans whom he had been instructed to call. Abel and Manes
sat in the cellar until the morning because Germans had no desire to
come in the middle of the night. They knocked on the trapdoor, but
Podorewski leaned down and told them to be quiet because it was too
dangerous for them to come out. So they sat there knowing nothing
until the last moment; Podorewski spared them this knowledge. . . .

The Jews were ghosts, thought Podorewski. They emerged from
under the ground at night and crept under the windows. The peasants
were ignorant and superstitious, a sin, they thought, not to help. But
Podorewski studied philosophy. Was it possible, he thought, to help
at all? Perhaps only by shortening the pain of living. . . . It was not a
matter of the money that would become his in the final result. He
had enough of his own. But, on the other hand, if it should fall into
the German hands, or go to the dogs. . . . He was a philosopher.

In the morning people saw how an old Jew with a small boy, his
grandson, were pushed onto the same truck that came for Abel and
Manes. The old Jew begged to be let go, saying he did not care about
himself, only about his grandson. "But what can we do if Hitler got
you Jews entered in his black book?" joked the gendarmes. "Besides,
how can we let you go? What would the people who betrayed you say?"

After what happened to Abel and Manes, Aron declared that one
had to have weapons to survive. Słoń was of the same opinion. But
how, in their situation, were they to get weapons?

"By joining the partisans," said Aron.

"What partisans? Isn't it enough for you to be a Jew? You want to
risk your life as a partisan as well?"

"I only want to have weapons," said Aron. "So that no son of a
bitch, be it landlord or peasant, can trap me like a mouse or drag me
to the Germans like a lamb to the slaughter."

"If that's what you want, go and look for your partisans," said
Słoń skeptically.

Aron looked around, made inquiries, and finally found a contact.
They looked him up and down, agreed that he was young and healthy,
and made an appointment with him at night, on the edge of the ham-

let. Aron went. As had been agreed, he took his warmest clothes, money, and all the best things he possessed. But he returned the same night—without the money or the clothes and barefoot.

"Well, what happened?" asked Słoń.

"They have enough partisans," answered Aron. "What they are short of is clothing, money, and weapons. . . ."

Toward the end of the winter Złatka came to the forest. She had been hiding with the Nusens, who had jumped out of the train without their children. According to the Nusens, the children were to have been pushed out first, but they resisted and screamed and did not let go of their mother. So, Frymka, Nusen's wife, jumped out first. She had thought that the children would then follow her. But, seeing their mother falling out of the moving train, the children became even more terrified and clung to the hands and legs of their father. In the meantime Złatka jumped, followed by somebody else, and shots were fired. People started yelling that the Germans would realize where people jumped from and would come and shoot everybody on the spot. Nusen did not know what to do. His wife was already outside and the train was beginning to accelerate. The children were holding on to the window frames and wouldn't let themselves be thrown out. People yelled that he should jump while there was time, and they would throw the children after him, that the children would resist less once they saw they had been left alone. Everybody was yelling and screaming. People helped him up to the window. He did not even remember when he hit the ground. When he came to his senses, he got up and, limping, tried to follow the train, then turned back to look for Frymka.

The Nusens and Złatka hid in a cellar at a peasant's to whom she had led them. To tell the truth, they had so much money that, if that peasant had refused to keep them, they would have easily found another. But the fact is that, when Złatka's money ran out, the Nusens threw her out. The peasant did not care who was paying him, but the Nusens got the impression that they were paying for Złatka. She went to seek shelter with another peasant with whom her father had left for safekeeping some bolts of fabric from his shop. But the peasant said he could give her back all the fabric but no shelter, because no amount of money would make him endanger the lives of his wife and children. Złatka took two lengths of cloth and turned back to the

Nusens, prepared to pay this way for her stay there for a time. But, while walking through the woods, she encountered a band of escaped Russian prisoners of war who raped her and robbed her of the cloth. Soon after, Biumek, on his way from the Sadowskis', saw her in the bushes on the edge of the forest and took her to his group. They gave her food and slept with her; she was their only woman. Once, when times were particularly hard, they asked her to give them part of the stock that her father had hidden with various people, but Złatka had become calculating and did not want to part with anything. Nutek, who knew with whom her father's goods were hidden, wrote a note in her name to the peasant, saying that Złatka asked to give the bearers of the note two suit lengths of good English woolens and anything else they needed. Nutek and Aron went there with the note, took the goods, and bartered them on their way back for lard and groats.

In the spring Nutek received Aryan papers from his wife and took a job as a railway lineman near Miłosna. At that time everybody who could afford it tried to obtain Aryan papers. It was not so much a matter of money as of "good appearance" and manner of speaking. But even without a good appearance, with such documents, one could go to Warsaw by a blacked-out night train and stay in an apartment that was not visited by anyone and had a lavatory and running water. And, even if no one could be found who would take you in and keep you in an apartment with a lavatory and running water, or if you did not have the money to go to the city and live there on your own, or lacked the courage to do such a thing, Aryan documents could be useful on the stretch of road between the forest and the hamlets where you had to go to get bread and on many other occasions.

That is why Słoń got in touch with a woman teacher in Dobre who supplied Aryan papers for a fairly modest fee. One paid as much as one could afford to cover her expenses and those of the organization for which she worked. Everybody paid except Słoń, not because he acted as a middleman but simply because he had no money at all.

Słoń brought a photographer to our dugout, and we all came out into the open in broad daylight. The photographer mounted his tripod in a small clearing and unfolded a white sheet that had to be held in place by a couple of people. He also had a bucket of clean water so one could shave and wash.

The camera pointed at the forest, but the trees were screened by the white sheet. Everybody in turn was stood in front of it, washed, combed, and—insofar as anyone was capable of it—smiling. While one person was being photographed, the others held the sheet in place behind his or her back, lifting or lowering it in accordance with the height of the person in front of the lens, so that nobody would see the forest behind the person's back.

Everybody was photographed, not just those who were to get documents. The photographer wanted this, and so did everybody else. This was important—you could read it from the faces as they stood against the white cloth, and from the fixed, tense looks as they gazed at the lens. As if they had suddenly realized that this might be the only thing that would remain—a silent face against a background of an empty white cloth, behind which the forest could not be seen.

Father ordered the documents for Mother. Afterward, under her pressure, he agreed to have a birth certificate made for me. She insisted that Father should have such documents, too, but in his view that was preposterous. Not because his appearance was so "bad"; he looked quite "good" in spite of his thick, black, almost purple hair. Much more distinctive were his manner of speaking and his behavior. He spoke a unique cross of the Mazovian peasant dialect and Jewish sing-song with simplified declensions. He did not know any other way of speaking Polish and did not need to in the past because he could make himself well understood anyway. He was only a man who performed all his manly duties. He did not spare himself, he earned his and our livelihood, and he took care of us. He tried whatever he could. Toward the end he even installed in the landlord's cowshed a dairy where he milked his own three cows. He chopped wood and carried water to the house, lined our wooden walls with straw for the winter, prepared clamps of potatoes, and in the spring planted them himself on a small, rented plot. We had never suffered from the cold and had always enough to eat. Occasionally, he would get irritated or even angry for some trifling reason, but he had a right to because he was a good father and cared only for us. He did not care what other people thought of him. Why should he? The decisive thing was money, anyway. He cared about money. He had intended to move to Mińsk Mazowiecki and open a dairy there. He spoke, moved, and looked the way he wanted, the way that was natural to him. He never even thought that he could or would need to do it differently. He never tried to be brave. He went wherever necessary anyway, found hiding places for us, and brought food. He went out so many times, although he was never sure if he would come back. He did the same after Mother and I had left, and he stayed behind in the forest with Grandpa and Grandma. He did it in spite of fear. Only later, when he remained completely alone, did he become less cautious, or perhaps he did not feel like being cautious anymore. . . .

On his *Kennkarte* he was smoothly combed, perhaps for the first time in his life. His cheeks were sunken as always, perhaps a little more than before, and his look from under the dense, uninterrupted line of eyebrows was blank. He said he would not go to Warsaw, for, even if he looked like a squire and spoke like a lawyer, he would not be able to pretend that he was somebody else. And, if he had to live there in a hole, listen to steps on the stairs, and be afraid all the time, he would rather remain here, among the trees where he felt safer than among people.

Father was also reluctant to allow Mother to take me to Warsaw.

"You'll perish with him," he said. "They will ask him a question, notice something, check him up, and you both will be done for. Go alone, alone you can save yourself."

"But what for? What would I save myself for?" asked Mother. "What good would it be if I saved myself alone?"

"He may survive here. Somebody is bound to survive. . . ."

"I won't leave him here."

"Why?"

"Because he'll be eaten up by the lice here. He is so small. . . ."

"I'll see to it that he gets food, don't worry. Or I'll leave him with a peasant if you think he might do better there."

So for the time being Mother went alone to look around, as Father put it, and he took me into hiding with a peasant family. The peasant's wife had consumption and was extremely thin. She never got up from her bed and waited for the spring, when most consumptive people die, as for salvation. She would ask me to sit by her bed, so that she could see me better, and then used to say, "Look how thin I am," producing her barely alive bones from under the eiderdown to convince me. "I am consumptive and will die soon," she said. "But you, you haven't got consumption, so why?" And she looked at me strangely. And I had to drink moonshine with the peasant. It was warm, straight from the still. They had no children, and only the three of us lived in the house. This was just before spring. And after the first thaws, the Commissions started again to roam the countryside, so in the daytime I had to hide in the fields or on the edge of the forest, and the peasant brought me back after dusk. Occasionally he even took me to another hamlet and tried to leave me there. But I ran after him and did not let him hide from me, so in the end he had to take me back. I did not see his wife die, because Uncle Aron appeared one night and took me back to Father, to the dugout.

After some time Aron came again, with a lady who addressed him as Janek. The weather was fine and quite warm. Father let me out of the dugout. He was unshaven, almost completely black.

"Just look at you, what a sight you are!" said the lady to Father.

Father was embarrassed. His trousers were partly unbuttoned and a piece of his underwear was sticking out. When we started to walk away, he called, "Well, won't you say goodbye to me, Son?"

Now it was I who became embarrassed. I turned back, took leave of him, and never saw him again.

Just a few weeks after I was taken out of the dugout, they were all pulled out—Grandma, Grandpa, both aunts and their brother, the one I never called uncle because he was too young. It was in broad daylight, so they were almost blinded when they came out.

I don't know how they were shot, my old poor grandma and my grandpa who wore a small Jewish peaked cap. Did they cry or call anyone? Perhaps God? And what did my young aunts with shorn heads say? Grandma probably did not say anything, only cried. Where they stood all together in a row? Did my aunts take between them their younger brother who, after months in the dark, must have gone blind? And a good thing that he could not see. Maybe they were shot in the back? A terrible but short pain and it's over. . . . So was it worthwhile to fear it for such a long time?

Father was not with them that day. By some merciful chance, he went to see Słoń about something, so, after it had happened, he stayed on with the group. They were joined by boys and girls who had managed to get out of the burning Warsaw ghetto with their hand guns, and by a few escaped Russian prisoners of war. After the incident in our dugout, they no longer hid underground. They lay in the bushes, sleeping on blankets and ground sheets with which they covered themselves when it rained. They lay close together, sharing the straw and the sheepskin coats, and at night warmed themselves by a campfire. Had they hidden in a dugout, none of them would have come out of the forest alive.

Now that they had weapons they used them whenever the need arose. Only Father did not want to touch them. He continued to visit our squire, with whom he still had a sheepskin, a sewing machine, and a bicycle, not to mention a certain amount of cash.

One day, however, Aron, Słoń, and two Russians went to the manor. Father, of course, knew nothing about it. They left one Russian on guard and knocked on the window. The squire's young brother-in-law, Czesław, let them in. They told him to open the larder. Czesław tried to pull the alarm cord, but Słoń, who had kept an eye on him, tripped him up and held him down on the floor. They took away a basket of eggs, two lumps of butter, forty bottles of vodka, and a pair of new chamois-leather boots. The boots were too tight, but Aron insisted that they fit him and put them on. However, on the way back, he had to take them off because he was unable to walk. And, since he had thrown away the clogs he had worn before, he again returned to the forest barefoot.

When Father learned what they had done, he quarreled with them and left. After that he lived alone. No one knew where he slept or how he managed. When he called on the squire, he was told that "partisans took everything away."

In the meantime, a conflict arose between the Jews and the Russians, who had their own leader and their own plans but no weapons. So one night they brought moonshine from a peasant, threw a binge-drinking party, and, when everybody fell asleep, cut the pistols from the belts of those who had them and went off.

From then on the area was even more restless than before, and eventually the Germans decided to make a roundup of the Russians. They did not find the Russians but stumbled at once upon the unarmed group of Jews. It was daytime, so the men were lying under their blankets and realized what was going on when the Germans were already emerging between the trees. Because the Germans were shooting from behind every tree, they ran toward a clearing, where a machine gun had been just waiting for them. . . . All were shot; only Aron and Słoń, who ran between the trees, managed to get away, Aron with a slight flesh wound in his back. Słoń helped him up a tree, where they both waited it out until nightfall. Also Biumek survived, because he was hiding then, with his child, at the Sadowskis'.

Biumek's youngest brother, Eli, who was sixteen, had been the whole time at Śliwa's cowshed, up under the thatch. But when summer came and the roof began to get hot, Eli complained of lack of air. He came to the Sadowskis' at night to see Biumek, complained about the heat and loneliness, and asked Biumek to take him to the forest, "to the partisans." Biumek forbade him even to think about it and told him sternly not to move from Śliwa's cowshed. Yet Eli went to the forest on his own and joined the group. He did that just two days before the roundup. At the time, apart from Biumek, Aron, and Słoń, Nutek also stayed alive, working as a lineman near Miłosna.

Father lived through the whole autumn and winter, until the next spring. If he had managed to last out for just another few months, he would have lived to see the entry of the Russians.

No one knows how he managed for so long. Alone. One night men of the underground Home Army spotted him outside of the hamlet. "A Jew? What shall we do with him?" One of the Sadowskis was among them and recognized Father, so they let him go.

He was slovenly, unshaven, and thin. He smelled of rain and mud. He must have looked awful. Heaven knows when he had last washed himself. Was he still aware that he was human?

He could not and never tried to overcome his inborn fear of and repulsion to weapons. He feared and despised the heathen eagerness for deciding about life and death. Had it not been for this, he might not have died from an ax of a bandit.

Someone was waiting for him on that last night when he dragged himself all alone along one of his usual paths, clutching a loaf of bread under his coat. It was a question of money. He was amazed. What money? And suddenly he remembered. All the money he had been saving all his life for the hour of need—for ransom. Ransom would have to be paid; he had always been aware of that. Therefore, he had gathered money, bowing and scraping, even falling flat on his face. What else could he have been doing? His back looked as if he had always feared a blow on the back of his head.

And he was proved right to have gathered money so persistently. He bought with it the bread he was holding under his coat. One can always count on money, he thought. Money proves that one is human. And if you get killed for it, you are not killed like an animal, but like a human being, for money. . . .

People say of him that it was his fault, that he was so calculating and believed in money, and that he did not try to overcome his repulsion to weapons. Were it not for this, he might not have perished from the odious ax of a bandit. He might have perished much earlier. . . .

Part II

Mother

At night we walked to the blacked-out station and boarded a blacked-out crowded train in which people spoke to us and we responded, encouraged by the fact that they could not see us. And, by the time we arrived at our destination, it was already daytime—a dusty, early morning on a railway station. Uncle Aron took me to a small café and ordered for me cocoa and a crescent roll, for these things still existed. . . .

Mother came running in, her coat unbuttoned. She had long red hair that she had never had before. I hardly recognized her in the hat with a veil covering her eyes. And, even afterward, when I did recognize her, I did not have the courage to embrace her. And, when I finally did, she in turn seemed frightened and pulled away from me. Then she took me by the hand, and we went out into beautiful paved streets, filled with the clanging of tram bells and the steps of people who walked behind us and toward us and did not pay any attention to us.

"Don't hang your head," Mother said.

"Are there people living up there?" I asked, looking at the rows of windows in the tall stone houses.

"Yes," she answered.

"So there are so many people here?"

"Oh yes, very many."

I had not imagined that there could be so many people still left in the world. How could I have? Since the time when our shtetl disappeared I had thought that nothing remained except the fields and forests where we were hiding, that towns had ceased to exist. In the

last place I had been, one only met people in exceptional circumstances, and here there were so many, and one did not have to be afraid
of them. Mother was walking next to me and even smiling. But her
smile was of the kind I could still remember from the days when we
went visiting. Thus, we must be visiting here, I thought.

Immediately after she brought me to the apartment—where luckily no one was in—Mother made a big fire, warmed a cauldron of
water, and then stood me in the cauldron and poured kerosene on my
head because there were more lice than hair on it; this was what had
made her so frightened when I had embraced her in the café. Then
she poured kerosene on all my clothes and threw them in the fire.

The place had a lavatory and running water. This was very important. It was something unavailable in the country and it meant that
one did not need to get out at all, or very rarely, and that one did not
need to show one's face to anyone. One could live in the place, drink
the water, go to the lavatory, and nobody would know. But Hanka,
the young woman with whom we were staying, thought that we
should go out, not avoid people, not hide, that we should walk, talk,
and look at people naturally so they would not notice any fear in us,
and no suspicion would cross their minds. Mother agreed with her
entirely.

They knew each other from Dobre. They both attended the teachers' training school in Radzymin. Mother had a grandfather there,
who owned a sawmill and lived a long and happy life. He lived long
enough to see me, his great-grandson, come into the world and hap-
pily enough managed to die before all this began. But Mother had
been unable to finish school. She had to leave it after one year. She
was claimed by the community of Dobre, which until the end remained loyal to their God, the tradition of their fathers, and their
way of life. The community could not allow a good daughter of a
pious Jewish family, especially one as lovely as my mother, to grow
into a non-Jew among Gentile friends and perhaps even go out with
Gentile boys. . . .

Didn't Hanka know, from the beginning, that I was circumcised?
Perhaps she had forgotten. Or perhaps, from the beginning, she was
against bringing me to her home. Or perhaps she had agreed to it at
first and only later lost her courage? Her friend, Mr. Kamil, taught
me every evening how to pray. He told me to say, "Our Father, who

art in heaven, hallowed be thy name, thy kingdom come, thy will be done, on earth as it is in heaven. . . ." And, "Hail Mary, full of grace, the Lord is with thee, blessed art thou among women and blessed is the fruit of thy womb. . . ." And later on, "I am the Lord thy God who brought thee out of the land of Egypt, the house of bondage." I repeated this after Mr. Kamil and, as Mr. Kamil was Czech, I thought we were talking Czech.

But this was not the only thing I learned. One day, coming in from the yard, I knocked at the door, since this was what good manners demanded, but when I came in I saw Hanka's face red from anger.

"Do you hear how he knocks?" she asked Mother.

I did not understand what that meant.

"You knock like a beggar!" exclaimed Hanka.

What she really meant was "like a Jew." It turned out that I did not know how to knock. I knocked too softly and too timidly. I did it this way because my knuckles hurt otherwise. A knock on the door had to be short and firm. I tried to learn this in earnest, and the knuckles of my fingers were always red.

Apart from this, we fared well in Hanka's place. We drank tea with saccharin. We spread margarine or soft cheese on bread. I liked the tea and, after a while, got used to the stinking cheese. I was taught how to peel potatoes very finely. I bought them myself in a nearby market square, where I earned the appreciation of the women stallholders.

"And whose little boy are you?" they asked me. To which I always answered, "My father's and mother's." And they said, "Bright boy. . . ."

The rest of my time I spent sharpening needles and twisting and waxing threads because our principal occupation was making ladies' sandals.

It was not difficult to make them. You took three strands of hemp and made a plait, which was then wound around one of its ends quite flat until the shape of a sole appeared. Then this was sewn up and reinforced with thick thread. The thread had to be strong, so you twisted several threads together and then waxed. But even more important was the sharpening of the needles because the hempen plait was hard and, by the time a sole had been finished, the needle had become completely blunt. So, while one set of needles was being used, another set would be sharpened on a whetstone on which you had to spit occasionally. Then you handed out the sharpened needles and collected the blunt ones.

The sandals had wooden wedges, which were bought in a shop and covered with linen. The inner soles were cut out of cardboard by Mr. Kamil. Between the cardboard inner and the hempen sole you glued pieces of colored cotton tape in combinations of two or three colors. The preparation of the glue, that is, the mixing of the chestnut flour with water, was also my task.

The sandals were really pretty. They were worn by even the most elegant ladies with red varnished toenails. The colored tapes cleverly crisscrossed their feet and the high wedges caused pinkish marks on their bare heels. They walked with a light, soft step on our discreet hempen soles. Hanka and Mother also wore them. Both looked good in those sandals and in their very short dresses during the Sunday strolls, on which they took me with them.

On these strolls I had to walk in front of them and the rest of the company—such were Hanka's instructions. It was unpleasant to walk like this because I did not always know where to go and was constantly turning my head to make sure that Mother and Hanka were still following me and that I had not lost them. But then Hanka would whisper something to Mother, and Mother would say, "Don't turn around!" Sometimes I would stop suddenly to take Mother's hand in mine for at least a moment. I could not understand why I always had to walk in front. I liked much better those Sundays when Hanka went visiting with Mr. Kamil, and I went to church and for a walk with Mother alone.

Mother preferred taking the tram to walking in the street. On the tram she always tried to get us to the front car, with the Germans. She looked attractive with her swept-up blond hair which, after being bleached several times, was no longer red. She wore a fashionable high-crown hat with a black mourning veil. It was forbidden to ride in the front car if you were not German, but Mother always waited near the first car, and usually one of the men in uniform would help her up the step. Mother always said that she was not German, so perhaps she had no right to be there. But the German would assure her that it was all right as long as he was with her. Then Mother would thank him and the German would reply that the pleasure was his. . . . She also tried to arrange that I would sit in a German's lap and that as many people as possible could see it. She explained that I loved uniforms because my father was a military man, an officer, now in German captivity, and although I was very little when he went to war, I could remember the uniform well. The Germans sighed in sympathy, some of them also had sons, whom they had not seen for a long time, and some of them were just my age. . . .

On Easter Mother said that she would like to take me to a church on the other side of the Vistula to show me Lord Jesus' grave. But, instead of the grave, we saw an enormous fire with clouds of smoke. The fire had been burning for several days now, and smoke could be seen even from the Praga side of the river, but Mother wanted me to see it from nearby.

"Look at it closely," she said. "And, remember, over there lived our aunts and uncles and your small cousins, same age as you are. Many of them. You wouldn't have liked to be there, would you?"

"No, I wouldn't. . . ."

"So remember once again, no one must know that you're a Jew! Ever!"

"Never?"

"Perhaps never. . . ."

I walked upright. I stopped turning my toes in. Mother told me to look people straight in the eyes. I did. I was a child and did not find it difficult. But what if I had been older? Like Mother, for instance? Could I have done it? Probably not. Just as the others couldn't. They did not look people in the eye and they perished. It was said that they had "Jewish eyes."

She always looked people straight in the eye. How did she manage? Because she was a mother. She felt what is so often ascribed to men, but is felt first of all by a woman who becomes a mother: that she had done and is doing something of the utmost importance, something that has to be done, and nothing can force her then to give in, even if the entire world with its savage threat of annihilation turns against her. Why is it that neither civilians nor the military take this force into account in their plans? This force of mothers?

One day, while walking "in front," I got lost. I did not turn at the corner of Ząbkowska Street but walked straight on. And, when I turned around, there was no one following, except strangers coming behind me and toward me, on every side of me. I called, "Mama!" and started running—in circles—because I did not know where to go. I ran in all directions and started to cry. Then I noticed that people were stopping and staring at me, so I ceased crying and just ran. The sun was blinding me, and the clatter of steps on the crowded pavement was deafening. My throat was tight with suppressed tears, and I felt a violent desire to scream, but I was not allowed to. *They* were just waiting for it. Who? I was not sure who, but I knew *they* were there, around me, everywhere, in the clatter of the feet on the pavement.

I knew because I had heard people talk about children abandoned in the streets, abandoned and betrayed. It happened more and more often, and people talked about it more and more often. Hanka, who always insisted that I should walk in front, told Mother that this was in case of a roundup in the street, but she must have wanted me to get lost. . . . She several times said to Mother, "Give the boy away somewhere, send him back, do something with him, or you'll perish with him and all of us will perish with you, there have been so many accidents because of children." "But he is such a clever and obedient child," Mother answered. "But a child, only a child! He may forget himself, and he is a boy. . . . You cannot put yourself and others in such danger! Alone you can survive, alone you are not so exposed, and you may stay with me as long as you wish, but this way. . . ." But Mother did not want to send me away, so Hanka arranged these walks with me "in front"—because I was circumcised. I was circumcised, and this is what I was thinking about when running around in despair among the Sunday crowd who should know nothing about it. Who must not and would not like to know. They would certainly not like to know, I thought, meeting again and again their absentminded looks. For what would they have done? Nothing. They could not have done anything. They would have to stop and look, which meant to participate in it. And certainly none of them would want any part of it. . . .

If I had only begun to cry, somebody would have become interested and asked me where my mother was. And if I replied that I did not know, they would take me to the police station. And while they would be taking me there, everybody would be looking and saying, "They've caught a Jewish kid again. . . ." Because by then they would have noticed that my hair was too dark, or my shoulders were too high, or my ears were sticking out too much. . . . And at the police station, they would check and know everything. Therefore, I did not cry. I was forbidden to because I was circumcised. I was even forbidden to look for my mother. I was lost, but had no right to look for her. . . .

Thus, when a gentleman in a hat showed an interest in me and asked me where my mother was, I replied that she was at home.

"And what are you doing here?" he asked.

So I answered that I was walking home and somehow could not find the right way.

"But why are you so frightened?" asked the gentleman.

"I am frightened that my mummy will be cross with me."

"And have you got a daddy?"

"No, only a mummy, because my daddy is in German captivity."

"Do you remember your address?"

"No, I don't," I said. "But I shall find my way if you kindly take me to the street market where they sell potatoes."

So the gentleman took me by the hand to the market where I so often bought potatoes for dinner.

"Are you sure you can find your way from here? Perhaps it would be better if I took you home and saw your mother?"

"Thank you very much, but I can find the way now, and I'll run along, because Mummy will really be cross that I have stayed out so long. . . ."

I jerked myself free and ran as fast as I could, turned the corner, and hid in a gateway.

When I got home, Mr. Kamil shut me inside the wardrobe. He said he was doing it to frighten my mother because she had not kept an eye on me. But there was no need to do it; she was frightened enough. She returned home running soon after me. She knelt on the floor and sobbed when Mr. Kamil let me out of the wardrobe, and Hanka stood by her and comforted her.

But soon afterward we had to pack our belongings and leave. It was in the afternoon, late in the afternoon. Had it happened in the morning, Mother might have found a solution. Both Hanka and Mr. Kamil were out, and it was one of the neighbors who said it. If it had been Hanka or Mr. Kamil who said it. . . . But no, Mr. Kamil would never had said it. And Hanka would have given us a few days' warning. She would have said that Mother had better find another place to stay or even given her an address herself. And if Hanka did not know such an address, perhaps Mr. Kamil would. But why weren't they home just at that time? Maybe they did not want to be? Maybe they did not see any solution for us?

A man came in and advised Mother to flee right away.

"To flee?" Mother seemed astonished. "But why? Have I done anything wrong that I have to flee?"

"You know very well why. Don't delay, just take the child and go while you can. We are giving you good advice, we don't wish you any harm."

"But I have no reason to flee," answered Mother. "I don't understand what people can be thinking about."

"Just as you like, but remember that we have warned you."

So immediately after the man had walked out Mother grabbed a small suitcase in one hand and my hand in the other, and we left. A warm May rain was drizzling, and it was much darker than usual at that hour. We rode in a tram—first one, then another. We had nowhere to go, so we rode back and forth. We did not try to get into a car reserved for the Germans, and I did not sit in anybody's lap, just on a seat next to Mother, who kept looking out of the window every time we crossed the bridge. For we were riding from one bank of the Vistula to the other, and the afternoon kept drawing in and the hour of the curfew was inevitably approaching. Finally, we got out near the bridge, and Mother said that we would have to go to the Vistula because there was no other solution left and it was probably not worth our while to go on like this. None of our relatives were alive. All of them must have perished, even babies. They all were dead, except us. . . . So why? Why should we be different? It couldn't be so terrible to die if all of them had done it? But I did not want to go to the Vistula. I was frightened. I begged her to go for just one more ride on the tram.

So we went on the tram to the end of the line, and we got out at the loop at Grochów. Dusk was falling, and the tram was turning into the depot. Another tram arrived, almost empty, and a lady with a gentleman got off.

"All right," said Mother. "We won't go to the river. We shall speak to these people and let them do with us whatever they like."

With these words she pulled me after her, and we walked up to the couple who had just gotten off the tram. When we approached,

Mother told them at once who we were and why we were there. She said that if they wanted to, they could help us, and, if not, they could take us to the Germans. The gentleman turned pale; the lady covered her mouth with her hand. Then the gentleman took off his hat and said his name was Orliński. He took Mother's suitcase and told us to follow them.

We could not stay with Mr. and Mrs. Orliński for long because it was not safe there. But it gave Mother time to look for a more suitable place. She borrowed some money from Mr. Orliński and went to Dobre. She walked from the train at night and then sneaked into the house of the teacher who had provided us with Aryan documents. From her she got the address of Esterka, Nutek's wife.

Esterka lived in a red house by the railway, where Nutek was a lineman. A huge man, he had been a cattle trader all his life. He could barely read or write but spoke the beautiful, authentic Mazovian dialect of the cattle markets and fairs, so he had no difficulty being a lineman near Miłosna, where no one knew him. Esterka said that she would have gladly taken Mother in if Mother had been alone or if I had been a girl. But, as it was, the most she could do was to inquire about a place if Mother was prepared to pay—a hiding place, of course, because no one would take a chance with a child, especially a boy. "Why didn't you leave him with his father?" she wondered. "It doesn't make sense. . . ."

So Mother once again boarded a train and then walked for half a night to the country to see people with whom Father had left money. She knocked on the window.

"Who is it?" asked a woman's voice.

"A friend."

"What friend?"

"Don't be afraid, Mrs. Kurowska, it's me. . . ."

"Jesus of Nazareth!" exclaimed Kurowska. "So you are still alive?! O merciful Jesus."

"Please help me, Mrs. Kurowska, me and my child, or we shall perish."

"But of course we shall help, why ever not? As much as we can. But what can we poor people do against such a scourge? I shall wake my man."

"Don't wake anyone, Mrs. Kurowska. I only want a little of the money my husband left with you. It's better that no one should know. . . ."

But Kurowski had already emerged from the recess, in his long johns with tape around the ankles and his eldest son, Wicek, behind him, and all of them stared at Mother, marveling that she was still alive.

"Money? What money? Ah, that money . . . my goodness, but there is nothing left. We would have given it to you, why not, we are honest people, but there is nothing left at all. Abram took it, all of it. He has been here three times maybe. . . ."

"More like four."

"Maybe four, and took everything away."

"And, whenever he came, he could warm himself, and we gave him bread to take with him. . . . And he took everything, to the last penny. We gave it back, why not, when a man is in such need. We don't wish to wrong anybody. . . ."

"But he wrote to me, I got a note through Aron, saying that he had left enough in case I and the child would need it."

"Ah, you're talking about that money?"

"Ah yeah, he left something," Kurowski began to remember. "But we were afraid to keep it here because times are so bad, so we took it to the squire for safekeeping. . . . It would be safer in the manor house, we thought."

"If that is so, I shall go there," said Mother.

"Where?"

"To the manor house."

"But how can you go there in the middle of the night? Have some sense, woman. Someone may spot you and, God forbid, a misfortune on all of us. . . . You better come to the recess, warm yourself, have some rest, and the wife will go to the manor herself and fetch the money, have no fear. . . ."

"And don't you go out until we call you," added Kurowski when Mother walked into the recess.

Mother heard the door creak as Kurowska left. She sat in the dark, waiting. Then suddenly she heard the door creak again, and someone else left. She listened intently as the door opened again, and someone stepped in, so heavily that the floor shook. Mother clung to the wall and put her ear to it. She heard whispers. "You go, Antoś. . . . Go and wait. . . ." She could not hear anything else distinctly except the name

Antoś several times more. She felt that she had to flee. She sneaked in the dark to the other side of the recess toward a small door to the hen cote. She took no heed of the alarm of the hens nor of the rain and wind. She only heard the muffled pounding that pursued her and the hissing whisper "Antoś. . . ." She was running from that sinister whisper, and from the pounding that was following her, which turned out to be the pounding in her breast, in her temples, and under her own feet.

After this incident, Esterka gave Mother some money, and Mother left her a note to Aron, who used to come to see Nutek, and in it she asked Father to repay. But we never learned if Father had managed to do it before Nutek perished and Esterka moved out of the area. She was not at home when two Germans came in and asked Nutek if he had a shovel. Nutek said he had. So they told him to take it and come along. Nutek thought that this was the end. He walked slowly alongside the fence in the direction they indicated, but, as soon as the fence came to an end, he suddenly turned the corner and ran straight ahead into the field. The Germans called, "Halt! Halt, or we shall fire!" But Nutek continued to run, so they knelt down, took aim, and shot him. People said that the Germans did not know the truth about Nutek, that they only wanted him to bury someone whom they had shot earlier, and were very angry afterward when they had to take care of two corpses instead of one.

The home of Mr. and Mrs. Orliński was not a safe place because they had two grown-up children, Wacek and Wera, who were visited by their friends. Some of the young men courted Mother, and she had to go out for walks with them. Young and elegant, they walked along the streets, both men and women in high-crowned hats. They did not order me to walk in the front. . . . They had been told that we were Orliński's relatives. They distributed illegal papers with good news that cheered everybody up. But Mrs. Orlińska always interfered when they asked Mother for help. "She has a child to care for and enough worries of her own," she would say.

Therefore, as soon as the days became warmer and one could start renting summer places in the country, Mr. Orliński went with Mother to Wołomin and got us a room at Stawki. This was a year before the Uprising in Warsaw in which both Mr. Orliński and his son, Wacek, lost their lives.

At the summer place we had as our neighbors a doctor's wife and her little son who was younger than I. Mother told me always to give in to him and always praised the sand castles he built, although they were much worse than mine. She also ordered me to be particularly careful during those games in the sand, as the boys had the habit of peeing on it to make it wet. I always remembered to be a well-brought-up and shy boy who did not expose himself, and the doctor's wife praised me for it.

The doctor's wife was occasionally visited by Mrs. Polkowska, a short, stocky woman who brought lard and other foods across the "green border." She kept persuading Mother to take me and go with her to the other side of the borderline. She said Mother wouldn't regret it because there is no scarcity of food there, and what they really needed there was anyone who could clandestinely teach their children to read and write Polish. As a teacher, Mother would get a room and board for both of us, and the farmers would take good care of us. The children have been for years deprived of schooling, and this is a great worry to everybody, said Polkowska. Mother explained to her that she simply did not have the courage to go away with a child to so distant and strange places where she did not know anybody. What did it matter, argued Polkowska. She knew full well how difficult things were in Warsaw, where food was a problem and life was becoming increasingly dangerous, especially for a woman alone with a child. "And are you sure you wouldn't rather be farther away, in a strange area, where no one knows you?" she asked, looking closely into Mother's eyes. She added that in such a time people preferred not to know one another, and one could sometimes count more on strangers, if only because there are more of them, and, therefore, it was easier to find a kind person among strangers than among those one knew.

Mother understood that Polkowska guessed many things and that she could count on her if she ever needed the help of a "kind stranger." But she did not want to hear any more about the peasants and countryside. She had enough of that. She was afraid and would have never agreed if she had not encountered in Wołomin a man dressed like an office worker and carrying a briefcase.

She met him in front of a shop. He smiled and said, "You remind me of someone."

"You must be mistaken," answered Mother.

"I don't think so. Didn't you have darker hair before?"

"No, never. True, it is slightly bleached, but that's because it's in the fashion now."

"There you are, fashion! I know a little about that. . . . You are not from here, are you?"

"No, only temporarily, staying with friends," said Mother, turning to go.

"Don't hurry, madam!" he said, holding her by the hand. "Let me walk you home!"

"Thank you very much, it's most kind of you, but unseemly. . . . What would my friends say?"

"So let's go to a café. I'd like to talk to you."

"But what do you want to talk to me about?"

"About various matters, perhaps about mutual friends?"

"Maybe another day, later, not now, I haven't got anything with me. . . . Not even my purse."

"All right then," said the man, after pondering for a while.

"Could we meet tomorrow perhaps?" suggested Mother.

"What do you mean, tomorrow?"

"When, then?"

"Right away, in half an hour! Go home, get your purse, and come back. I'll be waiting."

"But I won't be able to make it in half an hour. . . . Perhaps in an hour?"

"I am sure you'll manage, this is a small town. . . . And remember, you'd better come! I am very interested in this conversation and so should you be, don't you think? Be sure to come because, you know, Wołomin is a small town. . . ."

"I really don't understand what you have in mind. You must be mistaken," said Mother.

But the man was not mistaken. Mother remembered him, he used to come to Dobre, knew my grandfather well, and certainly must have remembered Mother. Luckily, we stayed at Stawki, on the other side of the railway line, and for two days Mother did not leave the house. On the third day Mrs. Polkowska arrived and was thrilled when Mother unexpectedly told her that she had decided to move.

We had to take a train to Małkinia, walk with the smugglers across a forest through which the border ran, and cross quietly and as quickly as possible over barbed wires pulled down in one place so low that even a woman with parcels and a long skirt that hid additional smuggled goods could step over. And one had to keep an eye on the back of the German who was standing with a rifle in the middle of a clearing. The German stood in this position only for a certain time, after which he turned around and fired if he saw anyone. This was the agreement between him and the women smugglers, and one had to abide by it with truly German precision. Moreover, the German who entered this agreement did not assume responsibility for the actions of any other German on duty in the area.

The women crossed themselves, ran out of the bushes where they had been waiting, stepped over the wires pulling up their skirts, and ran as fast as they could into the forest. They did not stop running until they were out of the prohibited zone. Then, exhausted, they fell to the ground and crossed themselves again, promising themselves and the Virgin Mary that they would never again go over this line. They made this promise after each successful crossing.

I ran with them through the forest. I did not let them down, I did not say a word. Only once I stopped at the sight of incredible quantities of mushrooms and berries growing there. I had a great desire to pick them, but an angry tug brought me back to order. We ran on, trampling the flesh of mushrooms and berries, of which there were so many because no one was allowed to pick them.

Later we rode on a cart and forded a river. The village was indeed very remote, and no one could possibly know us there. It was called Kończany, and it was a straggling village with dark trees leaning over a stream, giving it a melancholy outlook. Or perhaps it only seemed so to us because we knew this was our last refuge. Not because we foresaw that here everything would come to the final resolution and conclusion. We only knew for certain that there was no more escape for us from here. It was a dangerous game, the most dangerous we had attempted so far, and we would not have undertaken it if there had been any other way.

We stayed in the schoolhouse, which was occupied by the Polkowskis and the Kłodowskis. Polkowski was a cobbler and Kłodowski a blacksmith, and neither of them had his own cottage or land. The schoolhouse was the only brick building in the village. It was roomy and bright and had a red-tile roof. The Kłodowskis gave up a room for us, as a contribution for teaching their two girls.

The children did not come to school. It was we who came to them. The classes took place every week in a different cottage, and the hosts undertook to feed Mother and me. Classes were divided into two periods: morning and afternoon. When we arrived, we were given breakfast, and then the children assembled; when they went away we were given lunch. Then came the older children who were busy on the farm in the morning; when they left, we were given supper, after which we could return home. As for the farmers, some were richer, some poorer, and some women cooked well while others not so well, but we never went hungry.

The children used Russian exercise books and pencils left in the school by the "Soviets" who did not believe in God, arrested anyone wearing a tie or a hat, had communal kitchens and communal wives, and formed cooperatives. They had left a great many textbooks and exercise books with oblique lines in the school that they had built. Religious textbooks and holy pictures were supplied to Mother by the priest from Zaręby because she taught the children not only Polish and arithmetic but also the catechism, which she learned with them.

Once a month Mother traveled as far as Sokołów and fetched a letter from her husband, my father. "Dearest Zosia, I am longing so much to see you and our little son. I am fit and well and hope we shall see each other again soon," wrote my father, an officer of the cavalry, in my mother's own round handwriting. We also had his photograph: a fair-haired, smoothly combed man in uniform.

"But he's not an officer," remarked Kłodowski. "Only a sergeant. . . ."

"He was not an officer then," explained Mother. "He was promoted later."

"But these are not the insignia of the cavalry," persisted Kłodowski.

"A fat lot you know if it's cavalry or not!" Kłodowska butted in.

"Of course I know. Haven't I served in the army?"

"Oh yes, you have, shoeing the horses. . . ."

"So what? But I know uniforms!" insisted the blacksmith.

Mother had to be careful of every word, every gesture. Now it was no longer a question of walking in the street with head high or smiling at Germans in a tram. Now one had to be among people all the time. Talk to them, listen to them, eat with them, go to sleep and get up, pray, fast, and feast with them, be seen wherever they went, because people don't like those who keep apart, and talk a lot, because people don't like those who are silent and always suspect them of something.

So one couldn't shun people, avoid them, remain alone even for a moment. And one had to be on guard all the time so as not to make a mistake, a blunder, not to forget anything and to be natural and at ease. To improvise and always be ready to improvise—never get caught by surprise. Play a part that one did not have time to learn and to play it day after day, at any given moment, without an intermission for collecting thoughts, catching a breath, taking a look at one's true face. . . .

Sitting at the same table with people whose bread we ate and who told us everything about themselves, we paid them back by pretending and telling the stories Mother had invented. But I did not have to play a part. I had been primed so well that in the end I hardly distinguished between invention and truth. I had a dad who had served in Mińsk Mazowiecki, in the Seventh Regiment of the Uhlans, his name was Stefan, and he was as tall as a tree. I had a grandma who played the piano, and a grandpa who died of cancer, the illness of gentlefolk, and my mother was still in mourning for him. I did not need to invent myths like other children. I had one ready made and beautiful. My own mother supplied me with it daily, lived it with me, and spoke about it—with a straight face. She was my best companion and a partner in this childhood game of mine. In the autumn and winter evenings the women gathered to spin or knit sweaters, scarves, and stockings and the men to smoke and talk. During those long evenings when the women sat at their spinning wheels or bent over their needlework, and the men smoked their shag, we had to sit with them and listen to stories we would have preferred not to hear.

For that was the time when the last Jews hiding in the surrounding forests were being wiped out by cold, hunger, and by the hand of villains who believed that their bodies and souls contained gold. Or perhaps those were not even real villains. Perhaps they were just disoriented, misled, because it was no longer clear what was forbidden and what was not, and those people never had much opportunity to give thought to such matters. For them the word "forest" was always associated with loot, stolen timber, and animals. And in the forest people and animals look and act alike. None of the people telling stories in that warm, cozy cottage knew that it was we who were dying in those forests, we who were sitting among them, at the same table, invisible, horror stricken, and holding our breath.

For the Feast of Epiphany, a nativity play was presented with King Herod wearing a small Hitler moustache, white Death with a scythe, a black devil, shepherds, and donkeys. There was also a "Jew," who made comic faces exclaiming "Oy-vey!" He was wearing a beard and earlocks made of fringe, a small peaked cap, and a caftan in which he looked like my grandpa. Mother wept at night as she lay in bed next to me. And, in the morning, she ran to Zaręby, to the church, knelt at the confessional, and told the priest that she was alone in a world by which she was terrified, that she had a little son, which made her even more frightened, and she asked him to forgive her that she was not able to tell more, but just came to cry it out. . . .

A quite unexpected worry beset Mother when the blacksmith started making passes at her. She could hear quarreling from the Kłodowskis' room. At first Kłodowski just shouted drunkenly at his wife, but after a time, seeing that his advances were to no avail, he began to bring up in the quarrels "the strays" whom his wife kept in the house, without knowing who they were and where they had come from.

The situation was becoming increasingly serious. Finally, one day Kłodowska took Mother to the side and told her that she wished her well and personally did not care who Mother was because for her a human being who did no harm to anyone remained a human being no matter what; besides, she had grown fond of Mother and felt real compassion for her, but her husband was an unpredictable, narrow-minded, crazy drunkard, and it would be best for Mother to keep away from him. She was not turning her away—she would never forgive herself such a sin—but was just asking Mother to find another place to stay. She did not care about herself, as her own life was ruined anyway, but she needed peace at home for her children's sake, and it might also be safer for Mother to move. . . .

Mother was in despair. How could she, in her situation, remember that—in spite of all she had been through—she was still a woman, and only twenty-eight years old. She rushed to see the Polkowskis.

"Don't worry, Zosia," said Polkowski. "All this won't last long, believe me. And for the time being you'll have to rough it with us. The spare bed is narrow, but you'll manage on it with the boy. Most of our children sleep on the floor anyway, so we'll spread one more straw mattress for them, and when we move from here, as we'll certainly have to, you can stay in this place, and wait it out somehow." Saying that he hummed the ditty "Oh Zosia dear, my song is just for you. . . ." He hummed it whenever he saw her. He was tall and slim and repaired shoes and boots like a real cobbler, but he did not look like one, and I always imagined that my dad, the cavalryman in German captivity, must look like Polkowski.

When we slept at the Polkowskis', Mother sometimes woke me up in the night and asked me if I thought Father was still alive. We lay on a narrow wooden bed, and the Polkowski children rustled on the straw mattresses spread along the walls and mumbled in their sleep. They woke up before dawn and sniveled, "Mum, something to eat!" until Polkowska appeared from the second room in her white nightgown and, threading her way between the mattresses, inserted pieces of black bread in their mouths. After that we could hear munching and grunting, and everything quieted down again, while Mother and I lay with open eyes, intently listening to the restless gusts of wind rising time and again outside of the window. These were the only moments when we were alone.

Among the things that Polkowska brought across the green border were small and thin sheets printed on one side of the page. Polkowski gave them to Mother to read. Sometimes Kaczorowski, who worked in the post office in Zaręby, would call on Polkowski, and the two men would talk late into the night in the other room, sometimes arguing vehemently.

At that time the area was becoming very restless. Boys who during the winter would sometimes go away for a night of revelry now rarely returned home. Kłodowska's younger brother, Mundek, came home with a knife in his back. He did not even feel it because it was a frosty night. It was only in the morning, when everybody got up, that they saw that Mundek was lying in bedding that had turned red from his blood.

"The nationalists," said Polkowski. "There are lots of them in this area, people like the Nienałtowskis, Świerżewskis, and other such 'nobility' with crests nailed to the doors of their peasant huts. Ignorant like other peasants, yet they like to swagger and rule over others. Before the war they went all the way to Białystok to smash up Jewish shops, and even as far as Warsaw. One has to watch out for them. Sometimes they don't even understand what they are doing, but they act like savages let loose. The bandits; for them Poland means to beat and kill."

Mother ran even more often to the church, and talked to the priest, who supplied her with religious teaching materials for the classes. On Sundays she crossed herself—slightly, in the elegant Warsaw style— and took communion in a church crowded with people so that everyone could see. Neither did she neglect to ride to Sokołów for those letters that always began with: "My dearest Zosia, I am longing so much to see you and our little son. . . ."

One night in the early spring, Kaczorowski knocked on the window. Polkowski would not let anyone in, but Kaczorowski insisted, "Open up, it's me!" He had no jacket on and no cap. This time their talk did not last long. Polkowska immediately started to pack. "Don't be afraid, Zosia," said Polkowski, taking leave. "It won't be long now, only a little more courage!" And Polkowska assured Mother that in case of need she could always rely on Kłodowska, who was a good woman.

The Polkowskis fled just in time, so everybody said. Mother carefully bolted the door and listened in the night for steps behind the shutters. But the fact that we were alone had its good side as well. I could now completely undress so that Mother could rub an ointment all over my body when I got the itch, and later I rubbed it on her back when she caught the itch from me. We had to get rid of the rash as soon as possible, and no one could know about it because they might stop the classes and then who would provide for us? Moreover, who knows, they might say that the itch was a Jewish disease. . . . On the other hand, Mother's nightly wakefulness did not augur any good. Then one evening Kłodowska came in and told Mother not to sleep at home.

"What happened?" asked Mother, turning pale.

"Better not ask."

"The Germans? Have they found out about the classes?"

"No. . . ."

"What then?"

"I can't tell you much, but it's not the Germans."

Mother grew even paler.

"If it's not the Germans, then who? What have I done wrong? I have only taught the children. . . . What can they blame me for? A woman, alone and with a child. . . ."

"That's why I have come," said Kłodowska.

"I taught the children. . . . Have I taught them badly? I did the best I could. I even taught them to say their prayers."

"Please calm down and don't lose your head," said Kłodowska. "There are people who won't let you come to any harm. Just to be on the safe side, don't sleep for a few nights at home, because somebody has accused you . . ."

"Of what?"

"Somebody has said that not everything about you is as it should be. . . . That you are not the person you pretend to be. People can put two and two together, you know, they have eyes and they see. They say you are . . ."

Kłodowska looked her straight in the eye, and Mother thought that in a moment she'll hear the word she dreaded most of all words. But instead something like a slight and sad smile appeared on Kłodowska's lips.

"They say you are . . . a spy," she concluded. "But don't be frightened," she added softly. "I don't know who you are, but I, too, am a woman, and I can see that you only want to preserve your child's life and your own, a woman can see this at once. . . ."

Mother slept for a few nights in Zaręby, at Kłodowska's sister's, while I was taken to the Kłodowskis' and shared a bed with their little Tereska. She was two years younger than I, so when we pulled the blanket over our heads and played immodestly in the dark, I did not have to worry that she would recognize I was a Jew.

Most likely the priest had a great deal to do with the fact that Mother was left in peace. Only Kaczorowski perished. They came for him at night, not the Germans but his own mates. They had a grievance against him, people said. Perhaps because he had helped Polkowski to escape, or perhaps there was something more to it. After they led him out of the house, they searched the cellar, looking for something, but found a petite, thin Jewish woman who turned out to be his wife. No one knew what became of her.

As soon as the spring came, the children started to attend classes of catechism with the priest at the church in Zaręby. Mother was reluctant to send me, saying I was too young. But Kłodowska said, "Send him even if he's too young!" So Mother did.

Every morning we ran to Zaręby across dew-scented meadows. When the days grew warm, we ran barefoot. We picked buttercups and put them on the altar. In church we stood in two rows, and the mysterious little light over the altar watched over us from above. Figures with beards—which nobody else wore anymore—stared down at us from the walls, and the tall, stained-glass windows shimmered with the most beautiful colors.

The priest would come out in white surplice and, with dignified gestures, conduct the service over our bowed heads. The organ, attentive to his gestures, accompanied him with benevolent gentleness, and one could feel the effort with which it kept itself in check so as not to boom with all its hidden power. When the priest knelt down, a bluish smoke rose upward, veiling the faces of the saints with their aimlessly outstretched arms. The church was then filled with a scent that one never sensed at any of the meadows.

The priest told us stories about Abraham, Isaac, and Moses. He was young and looked graceful in his cassock reaching down to his ankles. He acknowledged each correct answer with a gentle look but bowed his head and looked pensive when the answer that he had expected was not forthcoming.

Unlike the other children, I could easily remember all the melodious-sounding names mentioned by the priest. The stories he told us were simple, but some of them were very painful. We took them to heart. We were glad that, unlike the people the priest was telling about, we did not hate, did not betray, and did not want to kill anybody. We were not so sure about appropriating somebody else's willow whistles, matchboxes, or colored crayons. . . . We were afraid of the devil who was always sneaking up on us behind our backs, and we had a bad feeling of guilt because of our inclination to play with our immodest parts. But worst of all was not telling the truth. Especially when someone, like I, had a truth that could not be disclosed to anybody and had to tell lies every day by the fact of one's very existence.

The most moving story was the one about Jesus, who, although he was the son of the Lord God himself, had to flee with his distressed young mother from the soldiers of Herod and to hide all along the way for fear of being betrayed—so soon after he was born and after accepting the tributes and gifts that people so readily offer to a newborn. Later, he returned and grew up to be the best and wisest of men, about whom he knew everything. He sympathized with them, especially with those who were weak, stupid, and small minded and even with those who were bad and dishonest. He tried to warn them about the nonsense of their dishonesty, by which, in the end, they brought only harm upon themselves. Because they did not understand it, he called the moment toward which they were proceeding the Last Judgment; the suffering that they brought upon themselves by spoiling their beautiful chance of life he called hell; the void or memory of the evil they had done to others he called damnation. He loved men and wanted to help them because he himself—despite being God—feared death no less than they did. But they did not believe him. People find it difficult to believe that anyone is better than they are and suspect others of everything but goodwill. "O you of little faith!" he cried out in despair, seeing that what was so simple for him was almost impossible for them. How many injustices he had suffered—even in those distant, naive times—for telling the truth and opening his heart too wide. Sometimes he wished simply to close his eyes and die and never to rise from the dead. And yet he did not do so. He did not forsake men, although he knew he would be betrayed by them and tormented to death. How could he not have known? He was God, and even a mere man guesses such things at once.

He had exceptional luck with people: only one in twelve turned out to be a traitor. This betrayal hurt him more than the other wounds, and once again he was near to doubting. He had to be more than human to endure. For, if he had doubted, one more torment would have been in vain. And who would then be left to bear witness to the whole truth, if even he, who had revealed most of it, were to give in like the others, become resigned, and step back? "No," he said. "I would rather be murdered by you. This is the price you'll have to

pay for your lack of faith, for your lack of belief in your own selves!"
He was God—this was why he could remain true to himself, even in
his defeat that he had foreseen. He calmly walked up on Golgotha
and calmly died for he knew he had done all he could. Not even God
could do more.

This story had to be memorized better than any other. The priest,
who wanted to implant it in our memory, asked us questions that had
to be answered from our place in the row. I was the only one whom
the priest invited to stand next to him, on the steps of the altar, and
answer facing the assembled children. This impressed the children
and they nicknamed me "the priest."

At home I asked Mother, "Why did they kill Jesus? Why did they
do it?"

"Who did?"

"The Jews."

"The Jews did it?"

"Yes, the Jews. . . ."

"I don't know, my child. But I think that, if he hadn't been born
among Jews, he would have been killed by non-Jews. . . ."

It was full spring then, the time when there was not much food in
the country, and one had to look for it in the meadows and along the
banks of streams. There were no more classes because the younger
children attended instruction from the priest, and the older ones were
needed in the farmyard and for minding the cattle in the pastures.
On my way back from church I picked sorrel in the meadows and later
collected dry twigs in the woods so that Mother could cook the sorrel.

Only the Nienałtowskis gave us meals now, but only every other
day and only in the afternoon when their boys were available for lessons. Other farmers occasionally asked us to help plant potatoes or
sent us a few eggs, some butter, or honey for what they said they still
"owed" us. On Mother's name day Nienałtowski's daughter, Kasia,
gave Mother a yeast cake. We also got a length of linen made on a
home loom and bleached in the sun so that Mother could have something to dress me in for my first communion.

I was to take communion being burdened with a sin since I was
not baptized. I told Mother that it was a mortal sin to conceal such
thing at confession and take communion. But she replied, "Do you
want me to be killed because of you?"

"I most certainly don't, but it's unthinkable that the priest would betray us," I said.

"If he had to baptize you, that would be enough," said Mother.

"So perhaps I won't go to confession?"

"You've got to go!"

"So perhaps I won't take communion?"

"You must take communion with the other children."

"And carry a mortal sin?"

"If you don't do it, or if you say anything you shouldn't, you'll commit an even greater sin, remember that!"

The church was filled with people dressed in their Sunday best, gentle and smiling. Their pious voices rose and fell to the accompaniment of the organ. They knelt down in unison and got up in unison, with their eyes gazing at the altar and at us who were kneeling in front of it. I had an outfit from the white linen given to us, with a large blue collar and a white sailor's hat with a blue ribbon. Later, in front of the church, where our proud mothers were waiting for us, the priest distributed holy pictures. Every child received one, but I was given two. . . . I carefully trod the ground, from which I was separated by my long, white stockings, and, in spite of my heavy sin, I felt like an angel.

That summer I grazed Nienałtowski's cows with the other boys. We made campfires in the fields and chased dogs and frogs, while the cows grazed quietly, without our assistance, between the blue of the sky and the green of the earth to which they had an unquestionable right and which they shared with the birds, ants, and ladybirds in a natural and simple way that seemed impossible among people. Oh Lord, how fortunate the cows were, and how good it was to mind them, I thought. There was a boy I heard about who, when all his family had been killed and he had been left completely alone, went to the country to mind cows. No one knew him, and he knew nobody there. He said that he didn't remember where he came from, or what his name was, and people did not ask him any questions. They gave him a place to sleep, a bowl for his food, and he spent all his time with the cows. And no one was more fortunate than he because in the end he really forgot his name and where he came from. Others who were just as lucky would later leave because they could not forget who they were or because someone still remembered them. But he stayed there forever.

We, however, had to stop grazing our cows, in the middle of the summer, because the Germans were approaching. They had big Belgian horses with blond manes, harnessed to heavily loaded wagons. "They still have lovely horses," people said in wonder. They knew that the horses would not help the Germans much, so why should they be sparing their admiration? But they hid their own horses and cows in the forest.

Some of the wagons stopped at Kłodowski's smithy, and the Germans wandered about. One of them showed up in Kłodowska's kitchen, where Mother was peeling potatoes for the Kłodowskis and for us. He asked for a glass of water and then sat down on a stool opposite Mother and leaning on his rifle watched Mother peeling potatoes, obviously not thinking of leaving.

"Does he intend to sit here forever?" asked Kłodowska. "Tell him to go away! To the war! Over there, *piff paff*. His colleagues have already left. *Kameraden!*"

The German looked at Kłodowska and said something.

"What did he say?" asked Kłodowska.

"He says he has had enough of war and doesn't want to fight anymore. . . ."

"He's had it a bit too late," said Kłodowska.

"He says it's so long since he's eaten a home-cooked meal."

"Tell him, if he had stayed at home with his wife, he would have had his home meals. But now he's bound to eat the dirt in the ground. . . ."

The German drew a bayonet from its sheath, reached for a potato, and began to peel it. Maybe he thought that Kłodowska had said he should help if he wanted to eat.

"Do you see the way he is looking at you?" said Kłodowska to Mother. "As if he really hasn't had a home-cooked meal for a long time. . . . What is he thinking about, the fool?"

Mother blushed, but it was not a blush of feminine modesty. She was faced by a German, who looked at her with greedy eyes. What the German was thinking about was obvious for all to see. But what Mother was thinking about he could never have guessed. . . .

Later, a motor car, painted green and brown, drove up to the schoolhouse. Hearing the motor, the German dropped the potato, grabbed his rifle, and ran out. A major got out of the car. He wanted someone to roast a duck for his dinner. According to Nienałtowski, who brought the duck, only Mother would know how to properly prepare and stuff a duck because she came from Warsaw. The major was in a hurry, so a few other women were called in to help, and the major returned to his car. I stood nearby and looked at the shiny peak of his cap, his well-polished high boot, and his silver epaulets. He noticed me, stopped at the car door, and waved at me, showing that he would take me for a ride in the car if I wanted. "Go on, go when the gentleman asks you!" the people standing in front of the schoolhouse called out to me. But I ran to the kitchen as fast as I could.

While the major was driving around inspecting the places where people were digging trenches and felling the wayside poplars as well as those by the stream—they were enormous and cut down they seemed even bigger than before—the women bustled in the kitchen where the air was thick with the smell of duck sizzling in hot fat. Everybody was anxious that the duck be ready in time for the major and that he should enjoy it.

And, in fact, the duck was excellent. The major was so pleased that he even asked Mother to help herself to a piece. But this was more than Mother could do. . . . So instead the major asked for some Russian songs to be sung for him.

"But we don't know any," the women explained. "We are not Russkis, we are Poles. . . ."

"Never mind, sing Russian songs!" the major insisted.

Afraid that the major may get cross, Nienałtowski sent for Kasia, who knew a Russian song about blossoming apple trees and pear trees. She sang it in Russian, haltingly, and carefully skipping any words that might offend the major.

All night long one could hear the distant booming of guns, and on the following day shrapnel flew over Kończany. Suddenly buildings began to burn at both ends of the village. People ran to fight the fire, but the Germans would not allow them to do it—it was not the shrapnel that set the village on fire.

Nienałtowski immediately collected some geese, bacon, and eggs and rushed with Mother to the Germans. They accepted the gifts and expressed their pleasure at the loyalty of the inhabitants, but, unfortunately, they said, the buildings must be burned down because they were obstructing the field of fire. So people rushed for more poultry, bacon, and eggs, which the Germans accepted again, but threw up their arms, saying that there was nothing they could do because war was war and orders were orders.

"So leave us the schoolhouse at least," begged the people. "At least that! It's large, strong, built of brick, with a tiled roof; fire won't touch it! It has an attic and cellars, it could give shelter to many families. . . ."

"All right," agreed the Germans. They couldn't promise, but they would see what could be done. For the time being, however, as they were not ungrateful, they would take the population under their care and not leave them to the mercy of the flames and the Bolsheviks. Thus, everyone was to leave the village under their military escort, taking all the cows. Horses were to be requisitioned, pigs and poultry loaded on army wagons.

The barns were burning fast and easy. So were the hayricks and the thatched roofs of cottages. As they were leaving the village, people looked back to see whose cottage was already on fire and whose not yet. This had happened many times before, all through the long history of these villages. But their incorrigible, overconfident inhabitants, blinded by their habits and nature, which led them each time anew to believe in the durability of their works and possessions, seemed completely taken aback, as if this was happening for the first time.

When we were quite away from the village, the schoolhouse—sprayed with gasoline no doubt—burst into bright tall flames and burned more spectacularly than any other building.

On the way the cows had been selected and handed over to the army. The same happened with people who were being sent to dig more and more trenches. The gendarmes at the crossroads were on the lookout for the younger men and women. Soldiers on horseback rode up and down on both sides of the road, nervously urging on their horses who, in turn, drove the people forward. "Where are you driving us?" asked the people, turning toward the horses' snouts.

The roar of guns was getting louder and smoke of gunfire could be seen on the horizon. "Where are you driving us? What do you need this crowd of women with children and these old folks for? Leave us behind here! You've taken everything away from us, so at least leave us alone!" people cried.

"They are driving us to perdition!" shouted Nienałtowski, who had left his horses and cows tethered in the forest. "Run, people, run!" he shouted. "If everybody starts running, they won't be able to cope! Run!"

But women with children did not want to risk it, and only Nienałtowski and two other old men started running.

"Halt!" called a soldier. He pulled in his reins, wrapped them around his wrist, and drew his rifle.

The two other men who had been running with Nienałtowski stopped and turned back, but Nienałtowski's navy blue cap could be seen jumping up and down in the ditch.

"Turn back, man!" called his wife.

"Turn back, Dad!" shouted Kasia.

The soldier did not fire, and put his rifle down. Everybody stopped and waited. Nienałtowski crept out of the ditch, doffed his cap, mopped his forehead with his sleeve, and wiped the dirt from his high boots. At that moment the soldier lifted his rifle again. . . . Nienałtowski opened his mouth as if he wanted to say something, but suddenly threw his cap down and started running again. The soldier fired two shots. . . . Nienałtowski's wife was allowed only to pick up the navy blue cap from the ground.

Now firing could be heard from all sides—not just the roaring of artillery but also the thin rifle shots—and no one could make out what direction the front was coming from. The women asked Mother to speak to the highest-ranking German and explain that we had nowhere to go since the firing was coming now from ahead of us as well, so why not let the people take shelter? The children had no more strength to walk. . . .

The German to whom Mother spoke looked down at us from his horse and pointed at me. Mother, without a word, helped me on to the saddle.

The horse was very tall. I nervously clung to its mobile neck, but Mother smiled at me from down below.

"Don't be afraid, be a brave boy! And thank the kind Mr. Soldier, he has a little son just like you. . . ."

The German was sitting well in the saddle, while I only on its upturned edge, so, when the horse lowered its head to crop a blade of grass, I hung over an open abyss. I then tried to grab hold of the German's jacket or trousers. Mother was walking by the stirrup, smiling and watching over me under the cover of her smile. She was watching over both of us, me and the German.

No one on that road was sure of their fate. But none of the people who happened to be there with us—with the possible exception of Kłodowska, who might have guessed it—knew that Mother and I were the only ones who had no right to walk *any* of those roads, not even driven like cattle. The people among whom we were born and with whom we had lived were dead by then. They had died along other, earlier roads while we were not with them. But they died under their own names, whereas, if we perished here, no one would even know who we were.

Yet Mother seemed no longer afraid of anything. Coolly and calmly she looked at the German who was letting me ride on his horse, and she talked to him casually, though when speaking German she had to constantly take care not to throw in any Yiddish word. Yet walking alongside the German who was carrying me on his horse, she no longer seemed concerned with it. Was she sure that we had won?

She held herself straight as she walked, as if not tired at all, and there was nothing coaxing in the smile with which she answered the German's remarks. On the contrary, she seemed to be saying: *Go on, ride along! You are no better than any other German; you just don't know what a German shouldn't know. . . . You are riding toward your destiny anyway, so why shouldn't you give my little boy a ride? He is so much smaller than you are, but the odds against him have been so much greater than they have ever been against you. So go on, carry him on your horse! That's the best you can do now.*

She watched me clutching the green cloth of his uniform each time the horse lowered its head, and said, "Don't be afraid, my son!" But the way she said it implied: "Don't be afraid of this German. He is not even cross when you tug at his lovely uniform. On the contrary, can't you see? He is glad, even pleased that he can have you in his saddle during his hour of uncertainty. . . . He is smiling, do you see? He is afraid. . . . So sit in his saddle, do it for him! For the moment, it's better this way for him and for us. . . ."

The front line from which we had been fleeing somehow turned out ahead of us. The Germans did not expect that. Before nightfall, airplanes flew in, and the sky grew dark as if overcast by a heavy cloud. Some of the planes lowered down, pouring a thick rain of bullets.

Somebody shouted, "Civilians, don't take cover!" So people did not hide, just dispersed in the field.

At dawn, a man in a light military tunic raked aside the sheaves among which we were sitting, and said, *"Zdrastvouyte!"*

At the roadside lay a horse, stitched to the green grass. We emerged on land washed clean with bullets. . . .

THE VICTORY

✿

Part I

The Russians came down the pitted clay highroad that went through village after village of which only the chimneys remained. They came through villages of jutting chimneys, sounding the road with long poles. They came on horse-drawn wagons, gun carriages, and slow, heavy tanks. Their heads were shaved clean, their dirty forage caps shoved back rakishly. The wooden spoons they'd made themselves stuck out from the soft creased tops of their boots. When they halted, they pulled out those spoons and ate their soup and kasha with them, then wiped them on their pants and stuck them back in their boot tops again. They advanced all day and all night and all the next day again until nightfall.

"My God, there's so many of them," the men would say uneasily. "No end to them."

The Russians were very young, eighteen-year-olds, seventeen-year-olds, even sixteen-year-olds.

"They've already lost all their regulars," the men remarked knowledgeably.

The young soldiers played accordions or harmonicas. They drank huge quantities of vodka, denatured alcohol, and cologne—whatever they could get their hands on. We heard they raped women the same way, but we didn't see anything like that. On the contrary, women looked at them with sympathy, even genuine feeling.

"They're still children," the women would say. "What do they know? What have they seen in their lives? They go off to war, they could be killed soon, and leave a mother crying at home."

We stood by the road and watched them while my mother stealthily wiped away her tears. From time to time she'd bend close to my ear and whisper, "We survived. You see, we survived it!"

I stared wide eyed at the tanks big as houses sweeping down the road and roadside.

"And what's going to happen now?" I asked, still staring at the tanks as they plowed the earth into crosscut furrows.

"Now things will go well for us. We'll be able to live like everybody else. And won't have to be afraid of anyone ever again."

"Won't have to be afraid? Why?"

"Because the war's just about over. You'll see, everything's going to change."

"And we won't be afraid of people anymore?" I asked mistrustfully.

"No, of course not. People will be good to us now. You'll see."

"But what about the Germans?"

"They're all gone. And they won't be coming back. We survived them! You understand! We've survived all those Germans."

I felt her warm breath on my cheek when she bent to my ear. Her cheeks were red, but not from the rouge she used to wear to look healthy and happy, but truly red.

"But why are you whispering everything in my ear?" I asked.

"We still can't talk about it openly. For the time being no one should know we're Jews."

"Then when?"

"When we go back to Dobre."

"To Dobre? Why do we have to go back to Dobre?"

"What do you mean, why? We must find your papa and grandma and grandpa, our family."

I didn't answer.

"Why don't you say anything? What do you think, are they still alive?"

Again I didn't answer.

"Why don't you answer me? Don't you remember them? Don't you even remember your papa?"

"I remember," I said. "But I don't want to . . ."

"What is it that you don't want?"

"I don't want to go back to Dobre. . . ."

"Why? Why not?"

I didn't answer.

"Why don't you want to go back to Dobre? Why don't you answer me? Say something."

"Because I don't want to be a Jew anymore."

Now she did not answer.

"Mama, didn't you hear what I said? I don't want to! I really don't . . . I don't want to be a Jew anymore, all right?"

Again she didn't answer. She raised her head but didn't look at me. She stared off into the distance.

"I won't be a Jew anymore, all right?"

"We'll see," she answered.

"No. I want to know for sure."

"Well, all right, all right, as you want. I won't force you. Who knows if there are even any Jews left."

In Kończany people were pulling metal locks, handles, grilles, and tabletops out of the ashes. They set up shanties in front of the gutted buildings and cooked in the open air. They ran around the forest looking for their sheep and cows. Some men went to the forest and never came back. Especially those who had made their happiness too clear when the Russians fled in 1941.

We walked from one fire-gutted ruin to another and said farewell to our hosts. They tried to stop us. Where will you go with a child? The war's not over yet and they've got nothing to eat in the cities. It's always easier here, in the country. It's summer, you can spend the night anywhere, even in haystacks, while people build their barns back up. By winter, a lot of huts will be livable again. Not everything's burned up in Świerże; you could stay there with somebody for now, and we'll send the children out for lessons. Who knows how long it'll be before they open up any schools. And what sort of schools they'll be. . . .

Only Kłodowska didn't try to stop my mother. My mother was sure that Kłodowska had guessed we were Jews but had tried not to let it show. For this, my mother loved her. She knew that Kłodowska had defended us from suspicion. Kłodowska's not trying to stop us only strengthened my mother's conviction that we ought to leave as fast as possible.

Both my mother and Kłodowska knew that the forest concealed not only sheep and cows but the partisans of the Narodówka as well. For them, Russians or Germans—one was as good as the other. With one difference—when it became known that the Germans weren't winning the war, the Narodówka began to fear the Russians more. And, besides Russians and Communists, the Narodówka hated the Jews. For us nothing could be worse. The Narodówka couldn't do anything to the Russians. And the Communists—as many of them as there were anyway—were hard to find. They never called themselves Communists. On the other hand, it was easy to find and catch Jews from Sokołów, Biała Podlaska, and the Białystok ghetto who were seeking refuge in the forest.

My mother knew all this. She knew who belonged to the Narodówka and what they did to the Jews. We had lived among those people and gone to church with them; my mother broke Nazi law to teach their children Polish and the catechism—they had no secrets from us. They said that the Jews had rejoiced when the Russians arrived in '39. They also said that the worst NKVD men were Jews. Some of them maintained that it was a good thing that Hitler annihilated the Jews in Poland before the Russians returned, otherwise, the Jews would have joined up with the Russians in annihilating the Poles. We heard that one all the time. It made my mother's flesh creep, but she had to listen and keep quiet or, if she spoke, to say the same things they did. It isn't hard to imagine what would have been in store for us if these people had found out we were Jews.

So, even when saying farewell, we weren't free to admit we were Jews. My mother felt guilty and impure when saying farewell to these people with whom we had lived through so much. She felt especially strange with people like the Nienałtowskis, who, in our last and most trying time, had aided us in a way that was both elegant and Christian by ordering additional lessons for their children so as to have another opportunity to feed us. As a woman and a mother, my mother couldn't help feeling grateful to the Nienałtowskis, while at the same time, as a Jew, she had been in constant terror of them. She was two persons at once and had to experience double feelings. There was nothing she could do about it. Saying goodbye to Kłodowska was the hardest for her. She broke into tears. Out of shame.

We traveled to the Bug River on a wagon. We crossed over on a ferry run by Russian combat engineers and made our way to a freight train packed with people.

On the train my mother again told no one that we were Jews. She'd only say that it had been a long time since she had had any news about her mother, father, sisters, and younger brother and that she didn't know what had happened to my father. She said her heart was troubled by the thought that something bad might have happened to them; so many bad things had happened after all. It made her sob when she talked about it. People comforted her as best they could. Every one of them had met with some misfortune, almost every one. But it wasn't the same for everyone, objected my mother. It's not as terrible when you lose someone, even if that person is near and dear to you, as when you lose everybody and you're left alone, all alone in the world. . . . Don't worry, don't worry, it can't be as bad as all that, people would comfort her, not knowing that she was a Jew and, for that reason, her worst fears could easily prove true.

In Mińsk Mazowiecki, my mother wanted to run and see the people she had known there to learn everything they knew, but she lost her courage and didn't visit anyone. In the trucks on which we hitched rides the soldiers tried to seduce her. When they got too insistent, she would say that she was the wife of an officer who had returned from Russia with the Polish army, that we had received news from him that he was safe and sound, and that we were now on our way to meet him. Only in the last truck, which was going to Dobre itself, did my mother say she was a Jew returning to the town where she was born, grew up, and where her family had lived. She asked the soldiers if any of them had met or at least heard of any Jews who had survived. No one answered her and no one tried to seduce her anymore.

My grandfather and grandmother, both my aunts, and my young uncle had had a very slim chance of surviving alone and without money in the forest. Anyone with some money could go from peasant to peasant and count on some sort of help. But you also had to know how to do it because having money had its bad side, too. You had to know who to go to, when, and how much to pay.

That wasn't for them. My grandfather was a religious Jew, almost a fanatic, and knew nothing of the world. My grandmother was smarter, but she was smart only in her own house, in Dobre, not in the forest. And they were both too old for that. My aunts, on the other hand, were too young. Basia was pretty, and a man from the Poznań area, a Catholic, had wanted to marry her and take her back there where no one would have known she was a Jew. But she didn't want to. She said that was no reason to get married. He proposed to

her again a couple of weeks before the Jews were deported from Dobre. Chańcia, older than Basia, was not only poor but ugly, and nobody wanted to marry her. She had thick legs and a long nose and
was afraid of people. Uncle Shebsl, Grandpa's only and beloved son,
had handsome *peyes* that fell onto his cheeks, childish and forever pale.
He wore a long Hasidic coat and a yarmulke on the top of his head
and studied the Talmud, although he was only thirteen years old.

Maybe my grandfather felt relief when the Germans lined them
up beside the dugout where they had hidden. Chańcia probably felt
fear and Basia contempt. Maybe both of them felt contempt when
they looked those men right in the eye. Maybe only thirteen-year-old
Uncle Shebsl was truly terrified. My grandmother must have been the
most unhappy, since she had toiled for them for years on end, her
whole life a mother. The Germans tossed them back into the dugout
where they had been discovered. Father, killed a year later, hacked
to death with an ax, was found by the roadside near Radoszyna and
buried there.

We stood in the center of the marketplace, surrounded by houses
and shops. The houses had the same old twisted shutters and the little
shops the same smoothly worn stone steps. The town square was dot-
ted with horse dung. When you stood in that square, you could see
all of Dobre. The church steeple pierced the clouds, and through the
gaps between houses you could see green meadows, sheaves stacked
in mown fields, forest. Everything looked just as it did when we sat
on a wagon loaded with our bundles and looked back one last time.
Only my grandfather's little fenced wooden cottage had burned down,
and the synagogue, which had once stood behind the first row of
houses, hidden from sight, had been torn down. Other than that, everything was just the same. Even the sheaves in the fields. There had
been only two harvests since we had left, the second was still in the
fields, while we had thought centuries had passed. People looked at
us as if we had returned from the hereafter and marveled—Can it be,
you're alive?

Those were new people. The people who had once lived here were
gone now. As if we had really returned after two hundred years, not
two. People stood around us and looked us over, and some kept running up to us to get a better look. They all expressed surprise that we

were still alive, to the point that we ourselves began to feel surprise, as if we had lived too long.

My mother looked around at the houses and little shops. She pointed to windows and called out names. When she had called out all the names of the shops, she began to point to the windows on the second floor and call out the names of the people who had once lived there. It looked as if she were giving a name to each of the houses, windows, and shops. No building in Dobre had more than two floors.

She neither wept nor grieved, and no one was surprised by that. You weep when someone close to you dies. You grieve when it's someone truly dear to you. But not when a town perishes. It wouldn't have been hard to imagine my mother's grief had only our family proved to have perished while all the others were still alive. If every second family had perished, ours included, then the tragedy would have been more understandable and you could grieve. Or, if one person from every family had survived and if all the survivors stood there in the marketplace, they could have wept together. Not even one person from every family, but from every second one. . . . But it wasn't that way! This was not the usual kind of human tragedy. This was beyond human measure. And, in such cases, a person cannot really feel or understand what has happened. This is how nature protects people.

So my mother did not weep, but, with tears in her eyes, she embraced our former enemy, Nusen, his wife, Frymka, and the Fryds because, of the whole town of Dobre, only the Nusens and the Fryds, with their son, Izak, who was my age, had survived. From the surrounding area, Aron, Słoń, Biumek, and his daughter, who was the same age as Izak and I, Bolek from Rudzienko, and, from Mińsk Mazowiecki, Adek and the Meinemers, relatives of the Fryds, had remained among the living.

The Fryds, it turned out, had been in Dobre all along. Before the deportation they had gone into hiding in a space beneath their own bakery and sat it out there. The whole two years. The Fryds, like all the other Jews in Dobre, had no idea where the Germans wished to deport them to. Neither had they known when and how the war would end. But, thinking logically, they decided that, when the Germans concluded they had deported enough Jews, they'd leave the rest of them alone. So they hid out beneath their bakery. They never expected they'd sit there two years. The baker's helper brought them food. Not the new baker, who mightn't have had any desire to see the Fryds survive, but his helper, who had gotten more money from Fryd than from the new owner, not only when he had worked for Fryd but also all that time when he was bringing them food. Providing them with food was no problem for a man who worked alone in the bakery every other night and who always had fresh bread right at hand. Had the Fryds been discovered, it probably wouldn't have been the baker's helper who'd have taken the consequences but rather the baker himself, whose fate didn't matter much to the helper. Every other night the Fryds could go out for half an hour, remove their refuse, and breathe some fresh air before going back underground again. They didn't get enough air and light. Izak's vision suffered badly because of that. Had they known it was going to last two years, they would surely never have done it. There was one good thing though—they never went hungry. They ate their own bread.

Frymka and Nusen, who jumped from a train to Treblinka, leaving their children behind, had survived by hiding with peasants. For money. But they never paid in advance and never stayed long in one place. They said that if you paid in advance, the peasant would try to get rid of you—any way he could. It was also dangerous to stay too long with any one peasant because, after a peasant had earned some money, he too would try to rid himself of any possible trouble. That's how Mrs. Fryd's sister and her husband had perished in Rudzienko. The person who was hiding them killed them himself. If the Nusens found an honest peasant, they couldn't stay long with him either because he would be afraid. Not of the Germans. It was unlikely that the Germans themselves would come looking for Jews. The peasant would be afraid of informers—his neighbors—envious peasant neighbors who grew jealous when someone else made money by hiding Jews. So when leaving a peasant's house, the Nusens never told him where they were going next. And, if something in their host's behavior wasn't to their liking, they'd steal away at night without his knowing it. They were alert, watchful, trusted no one. It wasn't enough just to have money, they'd say. You also had to be a merchant and know how to pay. If you couldn't do that, it cost you your life. . . .

"You got through the war with Aryan papers? With a child?" said Frymka with surprise. "Weren't you afraid the child would give you away? . . ." There was something unpleasant about her surprise.

Out of one hundred Jewish families, only the Fryds and the Nusens survived, but all the houses in Dobre were taken and we had no place to live. We had never had our own place in Dobre, because we had lived in Radoszyna and my grandfather's cottage had been burned down by the Germans after the typhus epidemic. However, my other grandfather, the one from Nowa Wieś, had owned one-fourth of a tenement in Dobre. He had never lived in it but had rented it to other Jews. That fourth of a tenement, built with Grandfather's money, consisted of a shop and living quarters that had a separate entrance in the rear. Another fourth of that same tenement belonged to the Nusens and the second floor to the Fryds. It was the best tenement in Dobre.

In our absence, when everybody had been convinced we were dead, that fourth of the tenement that legally belonged to us had been taken over by the Nusens, who had suddenly, God only knows how, turned out to be my grandfather's distant relatives. Nusen's own fourth, where his butcher shop used to be, was now a militia post, and a militiaman, Czyżewski, lived in the back with his family. The Nusens explained that they had had no way of knowing that my mother and I were alive, and nothing could be done now—it was too late. "We can't just go and tell the militia to clear out because we need the apartment for you! . . ."

It never occurred to my mother to try to oust the militia. Like all the Jews in Dobre, she dreaded any non-Jewish authority. She only wanted the Nusens to give up one of the rooms for us. The apartment was big enough for all of us. "How much room do we need after all we've been through?" my mother asked.

But the Nusens wouldn't hear of it. My mother asked the Fryds to intervene. The Fryds maintained that when the Nusens showed up in Dobre, they could have demanded to be admitted to their own apartment, but they hadn't done so. On the contrary, they had preferred to move into that fourth of the house that had belonged to my grandfather by pretending to be his sole living relatives, so they could assume possession of it while at the same time collecting rent on their own apartment from the Czyżewskis, with an eye to selling it.

When the Fryds' intervention didn't help, my mother appealed to Big Władek, the highest-ranking militiaman. She wouldn't have turned to any other non-Jew for help, but she knew that the Nusens as well as other Jews were much in debt to Władek from the time of the Occupation. Besides, everyone in Dobre trusted him. Władek heard my mother out and then had a little talk with Nusen in private, advising him that it would be better to voluntarily give us a room in the apartment, since a false deposition and pretending to have an inheritance not rightfully his were hanging over his head. The Nusens agreed to give us the room off the courtyard.

People said that somebody must have led the Germans to the dugout where my mother's family had been hiding. Maybe some peasant, maybe a gamekeeper. That was very likely, since the Germans were reluctant to enter the forest and certainly would not have gone there only to look for Jews. Too risky a business for such low stakes. They had to have had exact information, and that meant that somebody had informed. The Nusens and the Fryds thought that my mother should look into it, but my mother took no action. What difference did it make how it had happened or who had informed? She hadn't really believed that her parents, sisters, and brother could survive. So many others hadn't! How could you find who was guilty? And how could you prove that guilt? There had been no witnesses. In these things there never were. It was the Germans who had killed her family, she'd tell herself, so who else could be guilty? That's what she'd say—to justify herself.

It was different with my father. It wasn't the Germans who'd killed him. Neither could it be said that he had no chance of surviving. After all, he had fended for himself for such a long time. All he needed was only four more months. He was smart, shrewd, knew the area, and had money. The Germans would never have gotten him. There could be no justifying this. My mother had never been able to believe any of her family would survive but always hoped my father would. She went to Radoszyna.

The four-flat building where we had once lived had been burned to the ground. So had the manor, the granaries, and the barns. Only the brick cow barn was still standing. The Kurowskis lived there now. They were frightened by the sight of my mother.

"You're alive? . . ." My mother didn't like this question.

Kurowski led her to the place where my father had been buried. It was quite close, at the edge of a field. But the Kurowskis claimed that neither they nor anyone in Radoszyna knew who had "done it."

"Who had he come to see?" my mother asked. "He must have been here to see somebody, if it's right here that he was . . . that he was found."

"We don't know who he'd come to see," said Kurowski.

"He could only have come to see the squire, who had some things of his, or to see you, who had a thousand zlotys of his. . . ."

"Nine hundred, not a thousand," Kurowski's wife said.

"Let it be nine hundred. But he kept things and money only with the squire and with you because you were the only people he trusted, isn't that true? . . . Didn't he have money with you?"

"He did. But he took it all!"

"Not all of it."

"All of it!" shouted Kurowski's wife. "Every last bit of it!"

"Impossible. I used to get letters from him all the time, and he wrote me that he had left money with you especially for me."

"Bah, what he left . . ." Kurowski shrugged his shoulders.

"He left nothing," his wife corrected him immediately. "What could be left if he took something every time he came? . . ."

"So he did come to see you?"

"Seems he did."

"But that last time he didn't come to see you? Didn't even drop by? Why? Was he afraid of you?"

"God forbid! Why should he be?" cried Kurowski's wife. "Nobody here would have done him any harm. Sweet Jesus, no! . . . He must have been at the squire's, at Dziurewicz's."

"That's right," said Kurowski. "He could have had some business with the squire."

"Maybe he didn't even want anybody else to see him," Kurowski's wife added.

"I know he was at the squire's. The squire told me himself," my mother lied.

"So you see."

"But he also told me that he left to go see you."

"For what?"

"Because he needed money and didn't have any left at the squire's."

"It's hard to remember it all now," said Kurowski. "Maybe he was here. . . . But as for the money, like my wife says, he took it all! Down to the last zloty, all of it!"

"That's what we're telling you," Kurowski's wife continued. "He took it all! When he'd come, he'd warm himself up a bit by the fire, and nobody begrudged him bread either. Sometimes he even took some with him for the road. And nobody here ever did him any harm, as God is my witness! My God, the poor man. . . . In the morning people came running and said Abram's been killed. Some people went to see, but I couldn't bring myself to do it. . . . With an ax, oh God! . . . But it's good at least you're alive, and that you've saved the child."

"Who was he hiding with then?" asked my mother.

"Nobody knows. But it wasn't here, not in Radoszyna. They say he was hiding with somebody in Jacewek, but who, nobody knows. . . ."

"And where's Dziurewicz moved to?"

"To Mińsk Mazowiecki," answered Kurowski.

"Didn't you say that you'd been to see him?" said Kurowski's wife in surprise.

"Oh, yes, of course . . . I forgot."

"Maybe you'd like to stay here awhile, spend the night perhaps? Do you have a place to sleep?"

"No, no, I'm going back to Dobre."

"Maybe you'd like something to eat. You must be hungry from the road."

"No, no, I'm not hungry at all. . . ."

"Then maybe you'd like to rest up a little? We're living in the barn now, but it's been cleaned out, washed down, and rebuilt a little."

"Maybe some other time. I'd be better be going now."

"All by yourself? Aren't you afraid? God forbid anything bad should happen. . . . The times are so bad. . . . You better watch out. . . ."

The next day my mother went to Mińsk Mazowiecki. Dziurewicz's wife broke into tears when she saw her, but Dziurewicz looked sullen. True, my father had kept coming to his house for some time after my mother had gotten her Aryan papers and left for Warsaw. He'd take whatever he needed and had taken back almost everything. What he hadn't managed to retrieve had either burned down with the manor when the front passed through or else been carried off earlier by the partisans.

"Toward the end, he didn't come often because he was afraid. If there were no Germans in the manor, there were partisans, anybody who felt like it. . . . You had as much to fear from all those different partisans as from the Germans. . . ."

"But who did it?" asked my mother. "And for what? For a few paltry coins or the things people were keeping for him? He struggled so long, got through so much, only four months more and he'd be alive. . . . Who could have done it? Who had a reason to?"

"Better not look into it," Dziurewicz said. "What good can it do now? None. The times are still uncertain. . . . So many people were killed, even God himself doesn't know why. Why stick your neck out?"

"And what about justice? Is there no justice? There must be some justice. Aren't we entitled to any, my child and I? Isn't that what we survived for?"

"It's good that you yourself are alive, and that you managed to save your child. That's already some justice right there. And that'll make him rest easier in his grave. . . . He used to say he didn't know if he'd survive, but all he cared about was you and the child. Remember that. Think about yourself and the child. And nothing else!"

Mrs. Dziurewicz took my mother's prewar overcoat from the wardrobe and also gave her back our sewing machine, which they had with them in their apartment.

My mother brought the sewing machine back to Dobre and put it in the corner. She pulled up a chair, wrapped herself in the overcoat, pressed her head against the iron top of the sewing machine, and only then did she burst into tears.

Aron, Biumek, and Słoń sat out the end of the war in Drop at the Sobótkos', along with Bolek from Rudzienko, Adek from Mińsk Mazowiecki, and a dozen escaped Russian POWs. The Sobótkos had a mill on a cliff. A large, sound shelter had been dug into the cliff. The entrance was from the riverside and covered by thick bushes. The

Sobótkos cooked for them, and when there wasn't enough—it wasn't easy feeding so many men—they'd send them by night to the neighboring villages or still better to the manors, where, as partisans, they would "requisition" flour, kasha, vodka, and bacon, and this kept the Sobótkos supplied. The Sobótkos were no longer even operating their mill. The final weeks, when the front line was approaching, were the hardest. SS men were everywhere, nosing about like dogs. The gendarmes looked into every barn and granary, searching for cattle and grain. The gendarmes and SS men went to the woods to round up the cattle that had been driven there by the peasants. That meant trouble for the partisans, escaped Russian POWs, and the last of the Jews hiding there. The peasants wouldn't take in anybody for any amount of money. There was absolutely no place to hide either in the villages or in the woods, and it was then, right before the end, that many people perished. If it hadn't been for the Sobótkos, Aron, Biumek, and Słoń wouldn't have survived. During the final few days they weren't allowed even to stick their heads out of the shelter and relieved themselves right on the ground beneath their feet.

When the Russians finally arrived, there was a drinking bout at the Sobótkos' the likes of which had never been seen in Drop. The Sobótkos rolled a barrel of still-warm, undistilled home brew out in front of their house. Russians, Poles, and Jews drank until they passed out. The Jews especially. Then the NKVD came and confiscated everyone's weapons. They did nothing to the Sobótkos or the Jews. They only took away the Russians, who had escaped from POW camps and were drunk with happiness. It turned out that the NKVD had very little liking for their sort.

Aron and Słoń stayed on with the Sobótkos. Słoń was marrying the Sobótkos' daughter. Aron was going to marry a girl who had taken care of him when he was wounded escaping from a roundup and who was now pregnant. Biumek was engaged to Śliwa's daughter and was living with the Śliwas in Makówiec. Adek and Bolek were now in Mińsk Mazowiecki. Adek was hoping that a member of his family might turn up, and Bolek, who had some personal scores to settle in the area, joined the militia to get his hands back on a weapon. Aron, Biumek, and Słoń argued with him, especially on this point. They thought Bolek could cause them new troubles. And they'd had enough. They were well aware that none of their relatives were going to turn up. They were alone. Their decision was to start all over again. For the time being that mostly meant sitting around the Sobótkos' and drinking.

When Aron, Biumek, and Słoń found out we were alive, they came to Dobre to see us. All three of them wore quilted Russian jackets. Even Biumek's eight-year-old daughter, whose head had been shaved, was wearing one that hung down to the ground. Other than that they looked well and, with the exception of Aron, had a rather satisfied air about them. Their future fathers-in-law had already posted the banns and were inviting people to the weddings.

Not only were the three Christian peasant families who were marrying their daughters off to Aron, Biumek, and Słoń doing a "good deed" by making Aron, Biumek, and Słoń go to church and be baptized, but they also benefited by not having to give them any dowry. It was just the other way around. Biumek, for instance, who was marrying Śliwa's daughter—only ten years older than his own daughter—was giving Śliwa a farm in Makówiec with a large house, practically new, built just before the war. Having lost eight brothers and sisters, Biumek was now the sole heir to the family's properties in Makówiec, Rembertów, Radzymin, and Stara Miłosna. Although Aron and Słoń had very little property to recover, their future relatives considered they were doing well in marrying their daughters to them because Jews, even baptized ones, still remain Jews, meaning they don't drink themselves into poverty, don't beat their wives, and can always earn a living even without owning land.

The peasants from the surrounding villages and the people of Dobre were favorably inclined toward Aron, Biumek, and Słoń. They saw the step they were taking as the logical consequence of what had gone before. Some of them smiled ironically but, at bottom, they were pleased.

Nor did any of the Jews hold marrying Christians against them. Who else were they to marry? There wasn't anybody else. They had slept with these girls when they had no one else and when it made no sense to give any thought to such things since any girl could have been their last. They were indebted to Śliwa, the Sobótkos, and the girl who looked after Aron when he was wounded. They felt bad about having to convert, but what significance could that have after all that had happened? Even Fryd, the only one who went back to kosher food and who wore a hat when eating, didn't hold it against them. He just didn't accept the wedding invitation.

"Why not?" Słoń laughed. "It'll be a real Jewish wedding. So what if it's in a church? In all its days, Dobre's never seen so many Jews in a church!"

Biumek didn't laugh, whereas Aron was simply sorrowful. Aron had never thought we were still alive and that he'd meet up with my mother again. He was younger than my mother but had always wanted to marry her.

Aron, Biumek, and Słoń thought my father would have survived if he had taken their advice and stayed with them. But he always went his own way. They told him many times not to go to Radoszyna, but he was stubborn.

"He trusted the squire too much. And the other people he gave money to."

"Yes," my mother admitted. "He always trusted the people he paid."

But my mother was against any suspicion being directed at Squire Dziurewicz. He wouldn't have had a man killed for a few paltry things. Especially my father. Dziurewicz had never been pleasant or overly cordial to anyone, but he had truly liked my father. Maybe even more than the Christians he knew.

My mother didn't know what to think about the Kurowskis. She had a vivid memory of the night when she had slipped away from Warsaw and went to ask them for some of the money that my father had left with them and they had told her to wait in that back room. . . .

Aron maintained that it must have been somebody from Radoszyna who killed my father. Biumek, whose two brothers had been killed at Squire Podorewski's, suspected Dziurewicz. Only Słoń was of a different opinion. If my father had not been hiding in Radoszyna but in Jacewek, then somebody from Jacewek could have done it. It could have been the person who was hiding him, as Zduńczyk killed Mrs. Fryd's sister and brother-in-law, who were hiding with him in Rudzienko. But Aron, Biumek, and Słoń advised against making any accusations. If my mother accused an innocent person, that would be bad, and, if the person wasn't innocent, that could be even worse. They thought my mother should get out of Dobre as fast as possible, regardless of whether she intended to accuse anybody or not. The people guilty of my father's murder could be dangerous. Allied with their new families, the three of them felt safe, but even they were only waiting for the front line to move farther on so they could get out of there themselves.

Aron, Biumek, and Słoń didn't know with whom my father had been hiding in Jacewek. Or didn't want to say. But there was only one man with whom my father could have hidden there. His name was Wojtyński. He had not been my father's friend. More than once he had come to my father and said, "What do you need such an expensive overcoat for? Hitler's going to take it away from you anyway, better give it to me." When we were being expelled from Radoszyna, he came to ask my father to leave his money and all his better things with him. "You're going under anyway, what do you need it for? It'll all get lost and what good is that? Wouldn't it be better to leave it with me? If you survive, I'll give it back." Wojtyński was very angry when my father left nothing with him. He came in the night and hacked our shutters with an ax until all the glass went flying. Still, before we parted in the forest, my father said that as a last resort he'd go to Wojtyński's for the winter because Wojtyński wasn't afraid and was so greedy that it was enough to pay him well. So, when my father had no place left to go, he must have gone to Wojtyński's. Perhaps after a while Wojtyński had demanded more money and my father had to go to Radoszyna. Wojtyński followed him and waited until my father was on his way back. . . . Or maybe Wojtyński just waited at home for him. Then he could have put my father on a wagon, driven to that place outside Radoszyna, and thrown him off there so no suspicion would fall on him. Słowik, who owned that field, had told people of hearing something being thrown into his field that night. Słowik and the other peasants in Radoszyna were convinced that it had been done by somebody who had hidden my father and who then grew afraid he'd be found out.

Wojtyński might have done it not from hatred but out of fear. Not of the Germans but of the other people who were keeping my father's money and valuables. He might have thought they wouldn't forgive him for getting my father's money instead of them. That was four months before the Russians arrived, and he might also have feared that these people wouldn't forgive him for helping my father survive—no one had believed he could—and come back to claim his things. They might even have threatened Wojtyński. It wouldn't have been much trouble for them to send the Germans to his house, and that would have been that.

My mother didn't know what to do. She remembered the warning given her by Aron, Biumek, and Słoń.

Before my mother had come to any decision, somebody shot Squire Podorewski in Jadów. It was the same Podorewski from Piwki who had locked up Biumek's brothers, Abel and Manes, in a cellar when they came and asked him for food and had then called the Germans. He was found shot through the head in his apartment in Jadów, where he had been forced to move from the estate in Piwki.

The gun had been fired through the window, and no one knew who did it, but on the very next night about a dozen armed men came to the Sobótkos' in Drop searching for Aron, Biumek, and Słoń. They also asked about Bolek. Fortunately, Biumek was spending the night at Śliwa's in Makówiec. Słoń and Aron, who couldn't stand the lice in the house, were sleeping in the barn. But they had still kept the habit of vigilant sleep, so, when they heard something going on, they nudged open the rear door of the barn and fled into the fields.

They never came back to Drop again. They went to Bolek in Mińsk Mazowiecki and told him what had happened. Bolek went to the NKVD and requested a few militiamen with submachine guns and a truck. The militiamen went with Bolek around the area and shot anyone attempting to flee. They drove around in broad daylight. Bolek told them where to go and showed them the way. They shot Zduńczyk and Tomaszkiewicz as they attempted to flee. Bolek himself shot Tomaszkiewicz to avenge his mother. People said that he cold-bloodedly emptied a whole clip into him.

Aron and Słoń were terrified. "What are you doing!" they yelled to Bolek. "You're a Jew! You can't do things like that. Don't you understand? They'll never forgive you for it! Don't you know them? Even if you had shot personal enemies of theirs, they'd never forgive you. Because you're a Jew and these are their own people. . . . And not only you but all the other Jews will have to pay!"

"They won't forgive me? But I'm supposed to forgive them! . . .

For my mother, for Abel, for Manes, for the roundups? But you've already forgiven them!"

"What good is revenge? How can it help the dead? It can only bring more suffering to the living."

"And are they leaving you in peace? Didn't they come to Drop? They did, didn't they? . . . So what are you talking about? You don't believe it yourself and you know as well as I do that now they're afraid of what they've done. They're afraid of prison, of the NKVD. They'll try to kill anyone who can accuse them. So what are you waiting for? For them to get you and cut your throat?"

"There are other ways. You can catch them, arrest them, put them on trial. Let them rot in prison."

"They'll go to prison and they'll get out. Prison's no punishment!" answered Bolek.

Bolek was the son of Alter-Hill. They had owned a butcher shop in Rudzienko. One time a Volksdeutsch came to their shop and demanded meat. Bolek and his younger brother came out from behind the counter—a goddamn Volksdeutsch was going to take their meat from them? They beat him up and threw him out of the store. The Volksdeutsch informed the gendarmes. Two gendarmes arrived on motorcycles from Węgrów. Bolek and his brother hid in a neighbor's cellar; only Alter-Hill remained in the store. The gendarmes horsewhipped him and then ordered him to run. "Your sons ran away, now let's see what you can do. . . ." Alter-Hill ran out of the shop. One of the gendarmes shot at him, but his aim wasn't perfect. Alter-Hill lay dying on the market square and no one was allowed to go up to him.

Bolek and his brother had to flee from Rudzienko; only their mother remained behind to bury Alter-Hill. She then fell ill and had to be taken to the hospital in Węgrów, where she caught typhus. Running a high fever, she fled from the hospital to look for her sons. She got as far as Mińsk Mazowiecki. On foot, because no one would give her a ride in their wagon. But, before she arrived, the Jews had been deported from Mińsk Mazowiecki. Bolek and his brother, who were staying with relatives in Mińsk Mazowiecki, refused to be deported. When they were being taken to the train with the others, they started to run. Bolek's brother was shot in the back and died on the spot. Bolek managed to get away.

Crazed by grief, Bolek's mother was seen in the area for quite some time. She slept in the bushes, covering herself with leaves. When she went through a village, people sometimes threw her bread or called their dogs on her, but otherwise no harm was done her. Out of her mind, she walked around in broad daylight, and inevitably fell into the hands of a gendarme.

Tomaszkiewicz had neither killed her nor turned her in and was not guilty of her death. He was driving his wagon when a gendarme ordered him to stop and take the Jew, Bolek's mother, to Węgrów. It was late autumn. Tomaszkiewicz had no desire to travel so many miles in foul weather and didn't want to put his horse through it either. He asked the gendarme to shoot the Jew on the spot, in the woods nearby, and offered to bury her himself. Apparently he also treated the gendarme to some vodka.

Bolek knew that nothing would be done to Tomaszkiewicz if he were arrested. So they came at lunch, not in the morning, not at night. They didn't even force their way in. They simply knocked. "What's this all about?" asked Tomaszkiewicz's wife, stopping them in the front hallway. "We have an order to arrest citizen Stefan Tomaszkie-wicz," answered the sergeant. Hearing that, Tomaszkiewicz jumped out of the window into the garden. And Bolek was waiting right there, leaning against a tree, his finger on the trigger of his sub-machine gun.

People said that it was also Bolek who shot down Podorewski. But that later proved untrue. Podorewski had been killed by his own son-in-law, who didn't want him tried for collaboration with the Germans.

We put up new, very strong shutters and bolted the door at night with an iron bar. We were waiting for the front line to move farther away so we could leave. But the Russians made no progress. They even began coming back from the front for rest. A garrison was quartered in Dobre. This had its good side, as the area quieted down and we felt safer again.

Fryd was operating his bakery again, earning extra money by filling orders for the Russians. Nusen had somehow retrieved a machine for stitching leather that had belonged to his late brother, and the butcher now became a leather stitcher. He made boots for village cobblers and for peasants, who paid him in dairy products, poultry, and home brew. He swapped the home brew with the Russians for leather.

My mother took in dresses for alterations and repairs or traveled with other women to Lublin to buy yeast for Fryd and for the peasants who came to Dobre each Monday for the market. I started going to school. Aron, Biumek, and Słoń were baptized quietly with very few witnesses. Aron was married immediately after the baptism—his fiancée couldn't wait any longer. But Biumek's and Słoń's weddings were put off until Christmas.

Three Russian officers were quartered in our building; Lieutenants Etkin and Shteyn upstairs at the Fryds', and Captain Gopin downstairs at the Nusens'. Middle-aged, bald Gopin understood Polish and liked to sing Polish songs. He had a sunny disposition but always fell silent when he saw an NKVD cap. Lieutenant Etkin, who served at the quartermaster's and would bring home vodka and canned goods, was also good humored. Only Lieutenant Shteyn was silent and unsmiling. Tall and slender, he wore a well-fitted greatcoat made of English wool. For parade dress he wore white gloves and marched in the color guard. My mother and Mrs. Fryd would follow him with their eyes, trying to guess what he wanted, but Shteyn never needed anything. The three officers had been quartered in our building not only because it was the best in Dobre but also because we were Jews. Russian officers felt much more at home with Jews, and, although it made the apartments crowded, we all felt better having them there.

The officers brought us canned meat and fish, lump sugar, tea, and even American chocolate. Mrs. Fryd and Frymka cooked for them—pierogi, broth with noodles and beans, sometimes fish prepared Jewish style. They'd sit off to the side and watch the Russians bent over their plates eating Jewish food with gusto and military haste. The women would tell them how we'd outfoxed the Germans, and survived despite them, and how anxiously we had been waiting for them, the Russians, to come.

"Crush the Germans! No mercy for them!" they'd tell the Russians. "Kill every last one of them for everything they did to us! . . . Remember, have no pity, they shouldn't walk the face of this earth!"

On evenings when Etkin brought vodka home, Frymka, Mrs. Fryd, and my mother would prepare appetizers of sausage and pickle. The Russians would also invite their fellow officers quartered in the neighborhood as well as a soldier with an accordion. They'd urge everybody, including the Nusens, the Fryds, and my mother, to eat and drink with them. The Russians would be offended if anyone refused. So no one refused. The soldier would alternate playing lively and wistful tunes on his accordion, and the officers would either sing along, their voices dolefully hushed, or jump up, slap their thighs and boots, and race across the floor in a frantic Cossack dance.

When they grew tired, they'd ask for Jewish songs and dances. Then Frymka, who was the most musical, knew the most Jewish songs, and was also the heaviest drinker among the women, would walk out to the middle of the room. Bent at the waist, she danced looking down at her feet, flinging her head and arms about, and snapping her fingers. Everyone would pick up the beat and snap their fingers along with Frymka or clap their hands. One time, a little tipsy and in high spirits, Frymka called out for the Russians to dance with her. The Russians didn't have to be asked twice. They jumped out into the middle of the floor in their green shirts, their revolvers strapped to their waists, and laughingly began to imitate the passionate Hasidic gestures of religious rapture. Fryd, Mrs. Fryd, and my mother lowered their heads. Seeing this, Frymka came to her senses, covered her mouth with her hand, and burst into tears.

It often ended up like this even if none of the Russians tried to imitate Hasids with their eyes fixed on God. One word, one gesture, one tone of voice, one name carelessly spoken, was enough. If under the influence of the song, someone looked off into the distance then met someone else's eyes, that was enough to spoil the mood. The song would die in their throats, their arms would fall to their sides, and their bodies would shake with sobs, not the rhythms of the dance. Nusen would immediately take Frymka to their room and the Fryds would go back upstairs to their place; the Russians would put on their caps and leave, and only my mother had no one to cry her heart out with.

Sometimes quarrels would break out between my mother and Frymka, who, after the loss of her children, had become envious and ill tempered. The quarrels could start over anything, but they always ended the same way.

Everyone thought that Frymka shouldn't have jumped from the train without her children. But, of course, they never said so to her.

Frymka said she wanted to save them and everyone believed her. Who wouldn't want to save one's children? If she didn't save them, it means she couldn't. But still . . .

Frymka said they'd been shoved into a train so horribly packed that people were lying on top of one another and suffocating. So, when they managed to knock out the small, grated window, people were battling to get through as quick as they could. The opening was so small one couldn't squeeze through on his own, and people pushed one another, shouting, urging everyone to hurry. They promised Nusen and Frymka they'd throw out their children as soon as they themselves had jumped. So what else could they do? The guards had already started shooting. They had jumped, and, thanks to that, were still alive.

"Of course," my mother agreed, her tone conciliatory. "What good would not jumping have done? You would have all been killed. And how would that have helped the children?"

"And even if you had jumped with them," said Mrs. Fryd, "where could you have hidden with two little children? No peasant would have taken you. They wouldn't have been able to stand it in a hiding place, they'd have started crying."

But Frymka knew that Mrs. Fryd's son, Izak, though no older than her children, had been in a hiding place for two years and hadn't cried.

"The girl could have been put in a convent," my mother observed. "It would have been harder with the boy because he was circumcised, but they would have taken the girl."

"I wouldn't have given her to them!" Frymka shouted. "To have them raise her as a convert, an enemy? . . ."

"But she would have lived," said my mother.

"She would've lived, she would've lived! What makes you so smart all of a sudden? Didn't you leave your youngest boy at Stanisławów when you ran off to hide in the hay? . . . You think I don't know? You think people don't know about it?"

"Me, how can you say that?! I hid him with a Christian woman. The child had blue eyes and blond hair, he didn't look Jewish at all. No one would have ever guessed or noticed if someone hadn't informed. He was only a year and a half old, what was I supposed to do? Hide with him? In the hay? Nobody would have hidden me with such a small child, nobody! It would have been certain death. Should

I have let myself be taken with him? I had to think of my other one too, the older boy. And, thank God, he's still with me!"

"That little convert who kneels and prays by his bed every night?"

"So what if he prays? Praying doesn't hurt anybody."

"Praying to Jesus Christ?"

"He's still young; it doesn't matter who he prays to."

"But that's just what I didn't want. I could have gotten Aryan papers too if I'd wanted. Even before you got yours."

"You? But you look too Jewish."

"I look too Jewish? Look at her, I look too Jewish and she doesn't! You think I couldn't dye my hair!"

"What do you know? How can you know what I've been through? What do you know about living with Aryan papers? When you've got papers but no place to stay. And nothing to live on. No home, no family, no one in a world full of strangers. . . . You don't even have a real address. And just let them stop you and check it. Or check the boy to see if he's circumcised. . . . What then? And how about the roundups in the streets? And the blackmailers? And what if you suddenly run into somebody you know? All he has to do is call you by name. Just say one word, or show it on his face. Do you know how much courage it took to live on Aryan papers? To talk with people and let nothing slip? Never to say one more word than you had to. To be always on guard. Even in your sleep. To know when to go to church, when and where to pray, and say confession. And just how to say confession? People with Aryan papers perished right before my eyes! More of them were killed than those who hid with peasants or in the forest. It was easier for a woman by herself, but one with a child, a child who knew everything?"

"You mean you could do all that and I couldn't?"

"Then why didn't you?"

"Because I didn't want to! Can't you understand? Because I was a Jew and I still am! A Jew like all the rest!"

"So why did you jump? Why didn't you stay on the train like all the rest?"

"You begrudge me my life?"

"I don't begrudge you anything! But you envy me because I saved my child."

"No, you envy me. . . . And you know what you envy me for? My husband, that's what! You think I don't see how you look at him? . . . You think I don't know what you tell people, that it wasn't his fault. That it wasn't him who left the children, but me! That I'm the one that's to blame!"

"I never said anything of the sort to anybody. And I don't envy you your husband. I've never even so much as looked at him!"

"No? Why not? Because there's plenty of Russians around?"

Who knows how far they'd have gone if Fryd hadn't run over to them.

"It's shameful for Jewish women to talk like that!" cried Fryd. "How can this be? Is this what we survived for? Aren't you ashamed to let outsiders hear you? How can you stand there accusing each other? How can any one of us be to blame?! Stop it! This is shameful!"

Nusen took Frymka from the kitchen. The Fryds went upstairs. The Fryds were still a family and the Nusens at least had each other. But who would side with my mother? And so, after that quarrel it wasn't Frymka who cried but my mother.

My mother was still the best-looking woman in Dobre. And she was the best dressed, in clothing she remodeled herself; her dyed blond hair was very striking. The Russians courted her. And though they acted as military men are known to do, they were never vulgar or brash as they were with the other women in Dobre.

My mother was a widow, and the Russians were good to widows. Much better than they were to other women. In any case, they wouldn't harm a widow. On the contrary, they offered her help and protection. They weren't put off by her grief. There was a war on, and widows are common in wartime. "There's a lot of widows now," they would say. "And there'll be a lot more yet. . . ." They were good to widows because they were thinking of their own wives, who could very easily become widows themselves.

Captain Gopin increased his evening visits to us. He would smoke cigarettes and hum "My little drawer is kept under key, my keepsakes only for me to see. . . ." If the lieutenants were on duty, Gopin would bring his supper to our room and he kept staying later and later.

The captain was older than many officers of higher rank. He didn't have as many medals as the others but was greatly respected by the troops. My mother said that Gopin had also been through a lot, that he was the best Russian officer you could imagine, and that it wasn't his fault that he was still only a captain at his age.

Sometimes I'd fall asleep while Gopin was visiting us and wouldn't hear him leave. One morning I woke up and saw a shirt with captain's epaulets over the back of a chair and Gopin himself shaving in front of the mirror above our washbasin. That same day Gopin moved all his things from the Nusens' to our place.

Gopin liked to take me with him to meet his men. To win their captain's good graces, the soldiers would let me hold their weapons, so heavy they almost doubled me over. And they often treated me to vodka, which made me choke, but which I drank anyway. One day Gopin took me to the regimental bootmaker and ordered him to make me a pair of winter boots. I was very proud of those boots and of the fact that Captain Gopin was living with us. Even Frymka, my mother's worst enemy, suddenly began showing my mother respect and stopped quarreling with her.

After Gopin had moved in with my mother, Kola, an NKVD man, took to visiting us. No one knew his full name. He told people to call him Kola, and that's what they called him. Even though Kola didn't live in our building and never brought us any canned food, he was always treated to lunch or dinner whenever he came. He'd eat everything he was served and, if that wasn't enough, he'd call for seconds. Disregarding Gopin, he courted my mother. Also, in Gopin's presence he'd take me on his lap and have me repeat after him:

I'm a little flower, I'm a young pioneer,
I'm Stalin's little son, defender of the USSR.

Kola also taught Izak Fryd, who was more musical than I, to sing:

We'll go across Poland and across the whole world,
Until there's Soviet Republics in every land!

Fryd gave Izak a beating when he heard him singing that song in the house, and he questioned me whether any strangers had ever heard Izak singing it.

One time Fryd asked Kola what had happened to the Russian Jews when the Germans came to Russia. "What happened to the Jews of Kiev, Odessa, Homel, Saratov, Kharkov, Novgorod, Pskov?"

Everyone looked at Kola. No one said a word.

"They were evacuated . . ." said Etkin, finally.

"All of them?"

"Of course," said Etkin.

"And those who weren't evacuated joined the partisans," said Kola, the NKVD man.

"But the old people, the women, the children?"

"All of them," said Kola.

"Most of them were evacuated," seconded Lieutenant Etkin.

Gopin and Shteyn remained silent.

"In Russia the Germans didn't dare do the things they did here," said Kola, the NKVD man. "The people wouldn't let them! In Russia, Jew, non-Jew, it's all the same. How could they find out who was a Jew and who wasn't? They couldn't. In Russia people would never inform for the Germans."

"Still, most of them were evacuated," First Lieutenant Etkin repeated.

Gopin remained silent. Shteyn stood up and left the room.

Shteyn was a Jew. Mrs. Fryd invited him to spend Jewish New Year with us and the Nusens. She didn't invite any of the other Russian officers, not even Gopin. Lieutenant Shteyn, who never took part in any of the drinking bouts, accepted the invitation. When we were seated around the holiday table, he took three photographs in a cellophane envelope from his breast pocket.

"My mother," he said, handing the first photograph around. "My sister," he said of the second. "The young woman holding the child," he said, showing us the third photograph, "was my wife."

Shteyn was from Kiev, but his mother and sister had been living in Odessa. Like Odessa later on, Kiev was supposedly never to be surrendered to the Germans. The entire Ukrainian army had been massed to defend Kiev. And the entire army was cut off, surrounded, and captured. Afterward, some soldiers joined with the Germans. Shteyn's family had remained in Kiev, none of them having managed to get evacuated. None of the Jews who remained in Kiev survived.

Odessa, too, was defended. When it was taken by the Germans and Romanians, there were seventy thousand Jews there. When the Russians won back Odessa, they didn't find a single Jew alive—only corpses in the city's ancient subterranean catacombs.

The photographs passed from hand to hand in a circle around the festively set table. No one made any comment. Only shadows swayed on the walls as we rose before the lighted candles and Izak's father recited a prayer aloud.

One day Frymka and Nusen received a summons to Mińsk Mazowiecki, where, in strictest confidence, they were given party membership cards. They were told that from now on they had an obligation to inform the party about all suspicious goings-on in Dobre and especially about suspicious persons. The Nusens were taken by surprise. They had never requested to join the party, but they were afraid to refuse and so only timidly asked how they had earned such trust.

"Who else can we trust?" asked the party secretary. "The people who hate our Soviet liberators? The people who go to church and pray for our destruction? Or maybe those who hate the Jews?"

The last question struck the Nusens as the most convincing.

"Remember, if you're in any danger, there's no one to protect you but us, our power, our party!" the secretary said in farewell. "And so we must help each other."

Frymka held it against my mother that she had made no accusations in connection with my father's murder. She said that as the victim's wife and the mother of a child who was deprived of his father, my mother had an obligation to go to the NKVD and give them the names of all suspects. Then it would be the NKVD's task to determine who was guilty. That's what the NKVD was for. In Frymka's opinion, my mother's caution was common cowardice, and baseless, since the Russians were stationed in Dobre and there was no reason to be afraid. Sooner or later she'd have to leave Dobre anyway and so all the more reason to make an accusation.

Before long, my mother too was summoned to Mińsk Mazowiecki. But she didn't go. She was summoned a second time. In the end, Bolek came to Dobre. He was wearing a sergeant's uniform and had a medal on his chest. He showed my mother a list of names.

"What can you tell me about these people?" he asked.

"I can't tell you anything about them," my mother answered. "I wasn't here when everything happened."

"You can't tell me anything?" Bolek walked over to me and put his hand on my head. "You can't even tell me who murdered your child's father?"

"Leave me alone!" shouted my mother, bursting into tears. "What is it you all want from me? Haven't I been through enough in my life?! I don't want it! I don't want anything to do with any of this! I'm a woman and I just want to live like all other women! Don't I have the right to that? I don't want to hear any more about it! I've had enough!"

"Don't cry," said Bolek. "And don't be afraid. Why are you so fearful? You were so brave before. Because of your courage you survived. And now you're scared? Is this what you survived for? Stop being afraid! Times have changed, now it's their turn to be scared."

It took my mother a long time to calm down. Bolek walked over to her and placed his hand on her shoulder.

"If you're afraid, you can come to Mińsk Mazowiecki. In the truck that's waiting outside. Even right away!"

"What for? Who can I go to in Mińsk Mazowiecki?" My mother didn't understand.

"There's somebody there who could always protect you. Gopin? In a little while he'll be off to the front and what then? What will you do all alone with a child? Where will you go? I'm alone in the world, too, even more alone than you. We could be good for each other. You're the only woman I could ever marry. Nothing else matters to me. Do you understand?"

"Yes," answered my mother.

"So, how about it?"

"I'll think about it."

My mother understood Bolek very well. And she would have married anybody but him. She was afraid of him.

When Bolek left, my mother ran to see Ciokowa, the schoolteacher through whom Słoń had acquired Aryan papers for us, and told her every name on Bolek's list. To tell the truth, these weren't people who deserved her sympathy, but what mattered to my mother was that it be known in Dobre that she had nothing to do with the whole business and was even against it.

Dziurewicz's name wasn't among those my mother had seen on Bolek's list. But, the next day, Ciokowa came running over to tell my mother that Dziurewicz had been arrested in Mińsk Mazowiecki. Ciokowa, who was a personal friend of Mrs. Dziurewicz, insisted that my mother go to Mińsk Mazowiecki and save him.

"It'll make a good impression," she said. "And it might serve you well later on. . . ."

My mother was afraid to testify for Dziurewicz, but she was also afraid to refuse. She had always been very attached to Mrs. Dziurewicz and wanted to help her. On the other hand, although she didn't believe Dziurewicz had any part in my father's death, after all that had happened she couldn't be sure of anything anymore. But she couldn't refuse and went to Mińsk Mazowiecki, mostly because she was afraid not to.

The NKVD officer was glad my mother had come. He took a slip of paper out of his drawer and handed it to her. In a curving, schoolchild's script, someone had written that Dziurewicz, former squire of Radoszyna, had, like the majority of landowners, maintained good relations with the Germans, in exchange for which the Germans had protected his estate and property; that Dziurewicz, motivated by greed and innate anti-Semitism, had organized an attempt on the life of Abram—the son of Yehoshua of Nowa Wieś, of the Dobre community, county of Mińsk Mazowiecki—who, persecuted by the German occupiers, sought help from Dziurewicz. . . . And so on. Was she ready to put her signature to this statement?

"No, I am not!" said my mother. "I came to deny these charges. I know Dziurewicz, the former squire of Radoszyna, to be an honorable man who never did any harm to anybody. On the contrary, he kept us from being expelled from Radoszyna and afterward helped us as best he could. He hid all our things for us, he never refused us bread or milk when we'd come secretly to Radoszyna, and he even let us spend the night in the barn. Dziurewicz would never have done such a terrible thing to us. Not for the few paltry things we'd hidden with him and not out of any anti-Semitism either! The peasants were more anti-Semitic than the squire. How could anybody make such a declaration? After all, I'm a widow left without means, whose child is forever deprived of a father. Who could care more about seeing the murderer punished? I'll never forgive the man who killed my husband! If I had even the slightest suspicion about Dziurewicz, I'd have denounced him myself, but I can vouch for his innocence."

"You're certain this *landowner* is such a good man?"

"This is none of his doing. I'd stake my life on it."

"Watch out you don't lose that life you're so eager to stake," the NKVD official answered angrily.

My mother went straight from the NKVD to Bolek and said that if he really cared about her and wished her no harm, he'd go to the NKVD and make a declaration countering the accusation against Dziurewicz.

In the end, Dziurewicz was released. Everyone knew it was because of my mother and we immediately felt more comfortable in Dobre. Except that my mother quarreled with Frymka again because she had recognized Frymka's handwriting on the slip of paper the NKVD officer had asked her to sign.

It was announced that the seventh of November was to be a major holiday and was to be celebrated in Dobre. Ciokowa went to the priest for the key to the parish hall. But the priest had no desire to agree to, as he put it, an "atheist" celebration taking place in the parish hall. Ciokowa tried to convince him that the celebration wasn't going to be an atheistic holiday but a national, a Polish, one.

"Polish? . . . Aren't you ashamed to say such things? And to me, a priest? Do you think I don't know what November seventh is?"

"The date doesn't matter," said Ciokowa. "Please, believe me. There simply wasn't any other day to have it but the seventh. I can't tell you any more . . ."

"You should be ashamed of yourself for trying to fool your old priest. I may be old, but not that old. And I won't give you the key to the parish hall. I don't have it, I lost it," said the priest and crossed himself quickly.

Nothing further could be done. Ciokowa's husband, a local official, sent over Władek and two other militiamen. There really was no need for three of them. Big Władek gave one of the policemen his rifle to hold and, without even taking a running start, leaned hard against the door. It opened right up, some splinters flying off in the process.

My mother asked Ciokowa, as a favor to her, that I be allowed to recite a poem at the celebration. Ciokowa readily agreed and gave me to memorize a very long poem entitled "The Year 1918." My mother knew this poem from her own school days in Dobre.

Russian officers, schoolchildren, and militiamen wearing white-and-red armbands attended the celebration. The remaining places were filled by the populace of Dobre, who had been encouraged to attend by posters that announced in large letters CIRCUS PERFOR-MANCES.

The chairman gave the floor first to Major Motkov, the commandant of Dobre, and then to Ciokowa. Apart from the Russians, no one understood what Major Motkov said in his opening address, but from Ciokowa's speech it was apparent that there was no question of this being any godless celebration that could possibly discredit the five-hundred-year-old parish of Dobre.

"This is a holiday that all us Poles remember and know well," said Ciokowa. "One that will never be forgotten! A holiday that for a long time we weren't free to celebrate but that we're celebrating now and that we'll continue to celebrate despite all our enemies!"

This caused a stir.

"It's all the more pleasant for me," she continued, "that the Russian officers were so kind and so willing to come and partake of our"— Ciokowa placed full emphasis on the word "our"—"holiday." She paused and applause resounded. "Long live Poland!" cried Ciokowa.

"Long live Poland!" the audience responded, and the Russians applauded courteously.

"Long live this holiday"—Ciokowa again hesitated for a moment—"this holiday of November!"*

After the speeches, a piano was rolled onto the stage. The pianist, brought in from Mińsk Mazowiecki, wore a dark prewar suit with a white-and-red bow in his lapel. His hands clasped as if in prayer, he sang "Blossom My Rosemary" and "The White Roses' Buds Have Bloomed" and a few other songs that the Seventh Uhlan Cavalry Regiment, stationed in Mińsk Mazowiecki for many years, used to sing and so were known to every child in Dobre.

Every number on the program was announced both in Polish and

---

*November 11 was the Polish Independence Day since 1918.

in Russian. Ciokowa made the announcements in Polish, and a first lieutenant did them in Russian. When Ciokowa announced the poem "The Year 1918," the lieutenant bent to her ear.

"It's 1917," he said.

"No, 1918, I'm positive," answered Ciokowa, loudly.

"Well, 1918 was also important," the Russian agreed in the end.

The poem began with the words "Men, horses, cannons," and ended with the exclamation "We'll send our enemies hightailing it home!" This exclamation had to be delivered loud and clear, and with great conviction.

The audience listened to the poem in silence, paying it genuine attention. But, when I shouted, "We'll send our enemies hightailing it home!" people jumped up from their seats, clapping, stamping, and shouting "Bravo!" To the even greater delight of the audience, the Russians also laughed and applauded.

I didn't know what to do. I wanted to get off the stage as quickly as possible, but Ciokowa took me by the hand, led me back to the front of the stage, and told me to repeat the last stanza. When I had, Big Władek, in a leather jacket, rifle in hand, who had been standing off to the side the whole time, grabbed me up laughingly in his enormous hands and, holding me high above his head, carried me off the stage.

After the poem, Russian jugglers, a magician, and two acrobats also met with enthusiasm. In conclusion, Major Motkov, on behalf of the Russian command, expressed their sincere gratitude to Ciokowa for the excellently organized celebration, to the people of Dobre for attending, and for the fact that the celebration had occurred in such a friendly and cordial atmosphere.

That evening the Russians gave a party in our house. The rooms were lit by electric bulbs, which the Russian soldiers connected with long, thick cables to storage batteries placed in the courtyard. The tables were arranged in a horseshoe shape and a picture of Marshal Stalin, cut from a newspaper, was nailed to the wall. A colonel took a seat right beneath Stalin's picture. Russian women in uniform and representatives of the Polish militia also attended. Frymka, Mrs. Fryd, and my mother served the food.

The colonel proposed a toast, after which the Russian women intoned, "Let's drink to our motherland, let's drink to Stalin!" When everyone was tipsy, Kola, the NKVD man, called me over, stood me up on the table facing the picture on the wall and the colonel seated beneath it, and told me to recite "I'm a little flower, I'm a young pioneer, I'm Stalin's little son, defender of the USSR." The Russians were delighted, and Kola kissed me on both cheeks. And once again Big Władek, who was among the Polish authorities invited, stood up, took me from the table, and handed me to my mother. But this time there wasn't a trace of a smile on his face.

Big Władek was the tallest, strongest man in Dobre; people respected him, although no one was really afraid of him. Big Władek never did anyone any harm. During the Occupation he belonged to the Home Army but had no interest in politics; he only wanted to fight the Germans. When the Russians arrived, he came out of the forest. He had had enough of all that; he wanted to join a real army. But the army wouldn't take him because he limped from a wound that had damaged a nerve in his leg. So Władek, who could do nothing but bear arms, joined the militia. He had no intention of becoming a Communist. He said his only duty as a militiaman was to see that no harm was done to anyone in Dobre, and so no one should hold his joining the militia against him. On the contrary, he was the only militiaman people in Dobre liked. Even Frymka, who liked no one and the Home Army least of all, maintained that Big Władek was the only decent goy she had ever known.

Big Władek once saved the Nusens' lives. During the German Occupation there were many people in the countryside who'd take up arms by night and do as they willed. They'd settle their scores with neighbors, rivals, and anyone they didn't like. They took pleasure in having the power of life and death. Sometimes they joined the Home Army, sometimes other organizations, of which there were many at that time. When they needed arms, they'd attack Germans; when they wanted some fun, they'd attack the peasants or squires; and, if they met up with a Jew, they'd demand his money. All this was called partisan warfare.

A few armed farmhands once found Frymka and Nusen hiding in a peasant's storeroom. They threatened to inform the Germans if they weren't given money. The peasant was terrified they'd carry out their threat, but he didn't want to lose the money the Nusens were paying him. He asked the "partisans" to let him go with Nusen to see someone who was keeping money for Nusen and told them to treat themselves to vodka and snacks in the meantime. The peasant and Nusen set off, leaving Frymka behind as a hostage. Frymka would never tell what those "partisans" did to her in that time. The main thing was that the peasant returned with Big Władek instead of the money. Władek and his men disarmed the "partisans" and promised them that, if they so much as tried to squeal to the Germans, he'd find them soon enough.

Big Władek was always a hero to us children.

Gopin was promoted to major. The promotion came with his orders to depart for the front. Her face flushed, my mother packed Gopin's suitcase. She pressed his uniform, sewed his buttons on tight. She didn't know what else to do for him because Gopin was a man of few needs. She baked him cookies for the road. Once again Gopin took me to the regimental bootmaker and ordered another, bigger pair of boots for me, to grow into. As keepsakes, he gave me his compass, his binocular case, and his old captain's epaulets. He said goodbye to us and left but came back when it turned out that his departure had been delayed another hour. In the end, my mother put on her coat, got into the jeep with him, and accompanied him all the way to Mińsk Mazowiecki.

Two days later the Nusens left for Mińsk Mazowiecki and militiamen were given their place. This was my mother's idea because she felt uneasy in the large, empty apartment. The militia gave to the Czyżewskis the room that had once been Nusen's butcher shop. The back room with the kitchen, now at our sole disposal, was quite enough for us.

Słoń's marriage to the Sobótkos' daughter and Biumek's to Śliwa's daughter took place on the second day of Christmas. Peasants came in from all around. The marketplace was packed with wagons as on a market Monday. Even Major Motkov, who had remained in Dobre as the representative of the Russian command, took part in the show. He didn't set foot inside the church of course, but when the young couple came out, the major and his orderly, a Ukrainian known as the Grabber, and the militia fired their guns in a fearsome salute. Then Motkov and the Grabber got into their jeep while everyone else mounted their wagons, and all drove to Drop for the wedding party. My mother went too because Biumek and Słoń, as well as Aron, who was best man, had insisted. Only the Fryds refused to attend.

Aron, Biumek, and Słoń had invited all the militia from Dobre—just in case. The militiamen gladly accepted. Only Big Władek and one other man remained on duty in Dobre. Aron, Biumek, and Słoń had very much wanted Władek to come to the wedding party, but Władek said that with a bum leg he couldn't do much dancing anyway and he'd do more good at his post in Dobre.

About three hundred people attended the celebration. It was really a triple celebration because Aron hadn't had his own wedding party yet. The guests ate until they passed out and there was even more home brew than they could drink. The presence of the militia and Major Motkov kept things fully in control, and there were no fights. If, every so often, one man did accost another, it would end up with nothing more than a bloody nose; no knives were pulled. The orchestra alternated polkas, *oberkas,* and Cossack dances. The major and the militiamen danced as if possessed, and the Grabber, a cutup and crook, led the dancing. In the breaks between dances, everyone drank together. Anyone who had a gun fired it in salute and no one more often than the Grabber.

People drank to Biumek, who was now called Janek, to Słoń, now called Stach, and to Aron, who wasn't treated as the best man but as one of the grooms.

"Drink, Janek!" the guests shouted to Aron, who was also now called Janek. "After all, it's your wedding, too!"

"I never imagined my wedding would be like this," Aron said to my mother. He poured himself a full glass of vodka. He poured one for my mother, too. "Believe me, never like this," he said, draining the glass. He was drinking a lot. My mother was, too.

"What's the difference?" she said. "The most important thing is that you're having a wedding at all. That you're still alive. That we're all still alive."

"What good is that when our life's not what we wanted. And never will be."

"And was it ever what we wanted? No. And not only ours. Other people's lives aren't what they would have wanted either."

"Still, they always have it better than us."

"Stop it, Aron!" Słoń interrupted him. "This is a wedding."

"You hear him? This is a wedding!" Aron said to Biumek, who was sitting nearby with his head lowered. "This is a wedding party! What's wrong with you?"

"My brothers should be here," Biumek answered drunkenly. "My brothers . . ."

"Be quiet!" said Słoń. "Don't even think about it. It's over and done with! You've got to live! Life is tough. But is this what you survived for—to sit around and feel bad for the rest of your life? . . . And at your own wedding on top of it? *L'chaim!*"

"Now you stop it!" Aron shouted to Słoń. "You can't do everything you want! Not this anyway. Remember, you're not at a Jewish wedding and you never will be again."

Słoń was confused and lost his composure.

"All right," he said. "But get those looks off your faces, people can see."

"None of this does any good," Aron said to my mother. "We're Jews and we always will be, even if we're baptized twenty times. . . . Even if we don't want to be. We can't forget. That's something you can't forget. Besides, they'll remind us. Us and our poor, mongrel children. . . . And not just every once in a while either. . . . You'll see! Look over there," he said, pointing at the dancers. "I don't trust any of that. Maybe in a century or two. . . . Don't forget, as soon as the front moves on, we must leave here at once! And go far away. As far as possible. So far we can never come back."

While the drunken Major Motkov and the militiamen, led by the Grabber, were dancing with gusto, squatting and clicking their heels and using up their ammunition in salutes, a dozen or so armed men came to Dobre. They walked up to the militia post and fired several shots through the window.

"Open the door and come out with your hands up, and nothing will happen to you," they shouted in to Władek and the other man on duty.

"What is it? What do you want?" asked Władek.

"Don't ask any questions, do what you're told or you'll be sorry!"

"Don't open it!" shouted the other militiaman to Władek and loaded his rifle.

"What are you doing?" said Władek, grabbing the rifle from his hands. "Are you going to shoot at Poles?"

Władek opened the door and both of them stood there with their hands up. The men tied up their hands. They knocked the other militiaman unconscious with a rifle-butt blow to the head. They brought Władek out to the courtyard. They didn't hit him.

"Good thing you opened up," one of them said. "Could've been worse!"

They were standing under our window.

"Let me have a smoke, gentlemen," said Big Władek.

There was a long silence as he smoked.

"Just a little more . . . ?" asked Władek.

"Enough!" a voice ordered.

A shot barked out, and something splashed heavily in the mud.

A moment later I heard footsteps thumping on the stairs to the Fryds' place.

When the Fryds heard the shooting, they jumped out of bed and ran up to the attic. They pulled the ladder up and shut the trapdoor. They put everything they could find in the attic on top of the trapdoor.

The invaders didn't have time to try to get in to where the Fryds were hiding. But the next morning, everything in the Fryds' apartment was found torn and smashed.

But in our room only our windows had been broken and our shutters shot up. A jar of cooking oil on the window sill had been shattered by bullets, but no real effort had been made to break in. In the courtyard, where Big Władek's body had been found, there was some litter pressed into the mud and an unfinished cigarette.

The militiamen had left the wedding at dawn, tired and sleepy from a night of revelry and drinking. But it was noon when they returned to Dobre. All seven of them had been laid across a wagon pulled by a horse with no driver.

No bullets were found in their bodies. They had been cut up with knives and really had no faces left. They were taken from the wagon and laid out on straw in a shed. Their weapons and boots had been taken.

Witek Czyżewski came running up. His father was among the seven. "Come and see," he said to me.

The entrance to the shed was jammed. Women crying could be heard from a distance. People stepped aside to let Witek through. We approached on tiptoe.

"Third from the left," said Witek with pride.

"How do you know it's him?" I whispered.

"I recognize his pants."

Witek didn't cry. Neither in the shed, nor at the funeral. On the contrary, he seemed genuinely proud. His mother wept. All the women wept. But neither Witek nor the other children cried. If their mother were dying, they would have cried. Sometimes children cried when a father died. But it was very rare for a child to cry if his father was killed. Fathers were killed; nothing could be more normal. It made you interesting; it could be a source of pride. I didn't cry either when we found out that my father had been killed. It is true that we had lived apart from him for two years and I had managed to get used to thinking he was no longer with us. But I think I wouldn't have cried if I found out that Gopin, whose epaulets I wore, had been killed at the front. Children usually don't cry when their fathers are killed. Only later, when they've grown up.

But when Big Władek was buried, I cried.

Russian trucks arrived from Mińsk Mazowiecki with machine guns mounted on the cabs. The first thing they did was take away the militiaman who had been with Władek and whom the killers had let off with his life. No one knew what happened to him after that. He was never heard of again.

The NKVD ran from house to house. They shot Malczewski, the bookseller, who attempted to flee. Interrogations took place right on the spot, in Dobre, in the pretty schoolhouse that had been built just before the war. The bust of Marshal Pilsudski still stood in front of it. Ciokowa tried to intervene on behalf of Malczewski's sons. One was sixteen; the other only fourteen. People could hear them being beaten in there. But Ciokowa wasn't allowed into the building. She was told not to stick her nose into other people's business, or she'd be next.

The trucks pulled out, some toward Węgrów, others toward Jakubów. For two days shots could be heard from the forest. Right after the crackdown, Major Motkov was sent to the front lines. His orderly, the Grabber, never returned from the roundup near Jakubów. They tried to find his body, but he wasn't among those who had been shot. He vanished like a stone in water.

The day after the raid, the Fryds moved to Mińsk Mazowiecki. My mother couldn't do that. She wouldn't have anything to live on in Mińsk Mazowiecki. In Dobre we had at least our own apartment, and she could somehow support us by remodeling dresses and trading in yeast. But what could my mother do in Mińsk Mazowiecki, where there were shops that sold yeast and plenty of real dressmakers?

"We haven't done anything to anybody," my mother would say. "So what's there to be afraid of? We don't even have any money."

My mother told everyone that the attack had not been on us.

"They shot at our windows because they wanted to get in to the militia post. It's the post they wanted, not us."

Maybe they weren't really interested in us. But what did they want from the Fryds? The Fryds also hadn't done anyone any harm. Was it because they had money? But they weren't the only people in Dobre with money. Why didn't they go after the others? Why only the Fryds? And why wasn't anyone surprised at this? No one even asked why. Why wasn't even my mother surprised?

A lot of people in Dobre had money. The Jews had left everything behind. Buildings, shops, goods, furniture, utensils, clothing. My mother's cousins, the Szczepanskis, had left whole sacks of sugar and flour at Ciokowa's house, and Mrs. Fryd's father, Ajzyk, had left all his haberdashery goods with her. Ciokowa was an honest woman, and so, when Ajzyk or any of his family came in the night, they'd be given bread, sugar, ointments that stopped itching, and other medicine. But after Ajzyk got caught and Fryd's sister and brother were killed, no one came anymore. And the Szczepanskis never turned up—they had gone right to Treblinka.

And how much merchandise had been left with the Szczęsnys, the Zbrzeźnys, the Bodeckis? And how much with the Bóbrs? Once the black uniforms burst into Dobre and made a search at the Bóbrs'. They loaded up two trucks with merchandise. Bóbr's daughter, who was very good looking and well dressed, rode off with them. Half an hour later, the truck returned and the goods were unloaded.

The people of Dobre weren't monsters, and some of them sincerely sympathized with the Jews. But at bottom they were pleased. Even those who sympathized. So many places had opened up in town. So many goods. They couldn't help taking a quiet pleasure in this. Even the best of them, who found it hard to admit this to themselves. The Germans had known this and had certainly counted on it.

The Jews had left everything behind because they thought they'd be coming back. Those who fled from Stanisławów before the deportation to Treblinka would slip into the homes of people they knew late at night and exchange the last of their valuables for food and medicine. The drugstore in Dobre had done better than ever before. Other stores that used to be Jewish owned also did very well. The trade went on behind the Germans' backs. Food the peasants had hidden from the Germans came in from the countryside, and the women of Dobre would take it all the way to Warsaw. Textiles from Łódź were brought in through the "green border." The two largest Jewish ghettos were in Warsaw and Łódź. In these ghettos there were quite a few wealthy Jews who—with their backs, literally, to the wall— would exchange gold and other precious objects for a little food. So the people of Dobre had never been better dressed, had never eaten so well, had never lived in such good housing. And who returned to claim their things? And how many of the dresses brought to her for alteration did my mother recognize? Who came back to Dobre? Us, the Nusens, the Fryds. . . . Nobody else.

When after two years the Fryds came out of the hiding place beneath their bakery, that grave where they had been buried alive, they thought that after all they had suffered—almost the only Jews in the whole town to survive—everyone would have compassion for them, lend them encouragement, perhaps even rejoice that they were alive. But that night those armed men hadn't gone to anyone but the Fryds for money because the Fryds were Jews. And, if a Jew has money, everybody else thinks he's got the right to take it.

That's why I didn't want to be a Jew. I didn't want to be a Jew even more than before when I wasn't allowed to remember my father or my grandfather or my real name by which they called me or any word they had ever said to me. Even more than when the priest taught me how much harm the Jews had done to the world. . . . More than when we returned and people thought it strange for us to still be alive. And even more than when it turned out I could not even ask who killed my father.

Not only did I kneel by my bed and say my daily prayers but I wouldn't give up religious instruction, even though I no longer had to attend. I was the best student of religion in the class. Before classes I'd go to the school chapel with everyone else and sing hymns. And I would rise with everyone else after classes, make the sign of the cross, and say, "Thanks to thee, O God, for the light of this teaching. . . ." On Sunday I'd steal into church, where the people would peer at me, point me out to others with their eyes, and say, "Poor child. . . ." When the church was empty, I would kneel before the painted figures and ask them this once to use their almighty power and make me not be a Jew anymore. "Kind saints," I'd whisper, "isn't it enough that my father and my little brother and both my grandfathers and grand-mothers and all my aunts, uncles, and cousins were murdered? Who hadn't done anything wrong. Isn't that enough for you? What else do you want? Think about it! I am sure the Lord Jesus would never have approved of all that had been done. . . ."

One day the news came that Warsaw had finally been taken. And then Łódź, right afterward. We also learned that Gopin had been reduced to the ranks. He let some Home Army men go home after they had surrendered their weapons and he had not turned the men over to the NKVD.

Lieutenant Shteyn fell in battle outside Warsaw. The Fryds and the Nusens moved from Mińsk Mazowiecki to Łódź.

Part II

Dedicated to the memory of my stepfather, Asker Uszer Powazek

My mother didn't even try to sell our part of the building. That would only have rubbed people the wrong way and would have been dangerous. One time a Jew came back to Mińsk Mazowiecki to sell his house, and it cost him his life. People had gotten used to thinking that the previous owners were dead and that they now owned the houses where they lived. Although we were the only ones living in our part of the building, my mother would have been scared to leave Dobre carrying so much money. So she just sold her sewing machine and we left Dobre as soon as winter was over.

We went through Warsaw but didn't stop there. There were no buildings in Warsaw, only jagged, riddled walls; you could see the sky through them. We walked across a bridge where Russian women soldiers were directing traffic. There were no streets. Just footbridges thrown over mounds of rubble. Army trucks bounded over high humps of brick crushed by tanks.

Where the ghetto had burned, not even walls remained. Just level ground strewn with heaps of rubble. The road that had been dug through the rubble looked like a gorge in some exotic, stony landscape. My mother lowered her head so not to see.

In Łódź, the low gray buildings stood even and undamaged, all covered with prewar grime. The streetcar windows had been painted blue, but that only lent them a certain charm. There was a great deal of goods from American and English care packages in the shop windows; the streets and gutters were overflowing and pulsed with life. We stayed with the Nusens, the Fryds, and the Meinemer brothers and their sister Belcia from Mińsk Mazowiecki, who were all sharing an apartment with kitchen, bath, and four other rooms laid out in railroad style. Each of the rooms was furnished in a different color: coffee, cream, cocoa, and chocolate. There was a gleaming grand piano in the first room and the floors were a shiny parquet that squeaked slightly. Even the squire in Radoszyna had never lived like this. Or had furniture like this. The beds were wide, the mattresses springy. A night table with a reading lamp was placed beside each bed. There were dressing tables with large mirrors, each with its own soft, upholstered stool. On the sideboards, dressing tables, and bureaus sat porcelain figurines or heavy glass balls with fantastic forms inside them. The chandeliers dripped with crystals shaped like petals, triangles, and icicles. The walls were decorated with pictures and small hangings depicting chubby girls with angelic light blue eyes and boys dressed in snappy short pants, colorful little jackets, and caps. Other paintings and hangings depicted swans in love, roes, fauns, forest brooks, even gnomes. The hangings with German lettering had been placed upside down on the floor and were used for wiping your feet.

There had been many apartments like this when the Nusens and Fryds arrived in Łódź. They were almost completely untouched because they had been guarded by soldiers, and neither Russian nor Polish soldiers had any use for such things as these. The Russian men searched only for vodka, eau de cologne, and watches, while the Russian women soldiers were crazy about silk. They dressed up in long pink nightgowns, thinking they were evening dresses. The Polish soldiers guarding those apartments were only interested in money. A note on the door would say that the apartment had been taken by Corporal or Sergeant So-and-So, and everyone knew you had to find that corporal or sergeant, pay him a suitable sum, and then you could move in. Corporals were paid five hundred zlotys, sergeants a thousand. The quality of an apartment was also in keeping with the rank. You paid a sergeant a thousand zlotys, but you got an apartment like the one the Fryds, Nusens, and Meinemers lived in, with a telephone and a grand piano.

Izak Fryd and I rummaged through attics and cellars, where we found gas masks, army knapsacks and dressing cases, motorcycle goggles, bayonets, heaps of papers, snapshots, notebooks, books, and stamp albums. We peered at the people in the snapshots, the pictures on the postage stamps, and papers covered with illegible writing. We looked hard at the writing done quickly or slowly, carelessly or carefully, in pencil or in ink, black, blue, or green. When looking at these papers, we had the feeling that they were looking back at us with their silent, unintelligible, squinty letters, and this gave us the chills. After taking a good look, we'd tear the papers into shreds and poke the eyes out of the photographs.

We also smashed figurines of women in puffy crinolines, porcelain shepherds holding piccolos, and cups, glasses, and plates with chubby pink faces painted on them. We even broke the little gnomes. We'd hold up the glass balls to the light and look intently at the vague shapes shimmering inside them and then slam them against the concrete of the sidewalk. There was nothing really inside them. We even tore up some color pictures of marvelous African animals. All we kept was the army belts, gas masks, motorcycle goggles, and bayonets.

More and more people were coming to Łódź, where it was easier to start life over. And most of those who came were Jews. Izak and I would walk the streets, staring at everyone passing by. Whenever we saw a thin, pale person with large sad eyes, we'd step in front of him and ask, "Amkhu?" If they didn't know that Hebrew word, we'd excuse ourselves, and run off. But sometimes a person would stop and cry, "Yes, Amkhu!" We'd feel great joy. Proud of our success, we'd bring the person home, where he'd tell us where he was from and how he had managed to survive, and we'd do the same. So, no matter who the person was, there was always a lot to talk about. We kept searching the streets. It had become our passion.

We also searched through the rubble of the ghetto. Only the ghetto had been destroyed in Łódź. We combed through the half-buried cellars and ran into children who had once lived in those buildings. Considering everything we found there a relic, we brought home every rusted pot and broken candlestick. The stove lids we dug out of the rubble were set aside for fun. We'd attach a length of looped wire to them and roll them down the cobblestone streets, making a terrific racket.

It was there in the ruins of the ghetto, in a rubble-strewn cellar, that we found a German.

"A German!" we shouted. "A German!"

People came running, descended into the cellar, and pulled him out by his hair. His hair, which had not been cut for a long time, was long, but there was no stubble on his cheeks. Maybe he shaved every day or maybe he didn't even shave yet because he was too young. He was wearing a torn uniform and the blinding sun made him shut his eyes, then open them wide, though he still saw nothing. More people came running over.

"They've caught a German rat!" they shouted. "Look how he's afraid of the light! See, he can't open up his eyes."

They grabbed the German by his hair and feet and dragged him across the rubble. The German started to scream. Blood was flowing from his forehead near the hairline.

"Take him to the police!" people shouted. "To the police!"

The crowd was growing larger, and the German's screams also grew louder.

"Listen to him scream!" the people shouted. "But when they were murdering our people there was no screaming."

The German howled as if possessed. His screams were hard to bear. Unable to stand them any longer, someone threw a hunk of brick at him. Others bent down to get bricks. The people who had been dragging the German now moved off to the side. Everyone picked up bricks. The German quieted down, then grew completely still. No one said anything, they just kept throwing, the only sound the dry crashing of bricks. When the police arrived, there was a heap of bricks where the screaming German had been, a heap of rubble like anywhere else.

The next day we stopped on the street a little boy with glasses. We didn't know him. We asked him who he was. Frightened, he started screaming in a terrible, guttural voice.

"A German!" we shouted. "A German!"

All the kids from the street surrounded him. We pushed him up against a wall and started punching him. We kicked him and pulled his hair, tearing some out. His glasses fell to the ground and we trampled them to pieces. His eyes blank with terror, he kept screaming those same unintelligible sounds. The blood from his nose streamed into his open mouth, and, still screaming, he swallowed it. Choking, he called even more desperately and covered his head with his hands.

"What are you hoodlums doing?" people on the street started shouting. "That's a child you're beating up!"

"He's a German!" we shouted back. "A German!"

"A German? . . . But he's still a child."

"He's a German!" we replied. "A German!"

"That's good then," some of them said. "Give it to him, give it to him good! Didn't they kill our children? Give it to him, let him have it!"

So we beat him all the fiercer. We fought among ourselves to get as close to him as possible and hit him the most. Suddenly a woman came running out of a gateway.

"What are you people doing?! For God's sake, have mercy! That's no German, that's my son! My poor child, he's a mute! Don't you have God in your hearts?" She picked the boy up, stroking his hair already streaked with blood.

We looked helplessly at her. "We didn't know. . . . We thought he was a German."

I no longer bore a grudge against God for being been born a Jew. Now I was glad not to have been born German, and thanked him for it every day.

The Nusens, Fryds, and Meinemers had a stand with textiles at the Green Market. The market did a lot of business and so did the Nusens, Fryds, and Meinemers. The men brought in heavy bales of textiles on a two-wheeled wagon, which they pulled themselves, harnessed like horses, while the women stayed at the stand and sold the goods. When the men weren't busy transporting textiles, they stayed at the stand, too, throwing heavy bolts of homespun wool and linen for bedclothes and shirts onto a table, measuring out pieces with wooden yardsticks, and cutting the fabric.

My mother helped out by going to the wholesale dealers and manufacturers in Zgierz and Pabianice and ordering goods. These manufacturers produced linen and wool in small factories that operated a few looms, at most a dozen or so, but they worked day and night, producing much more than they were allowed to. These factories were run by the Jews who had formerly owned them or, as was often the case, had inherited them from relatives who had been killed. By the amount of merchandise for sale at the Green Market, the authorities could easily have seen that the factories were producing more than they were registering, but they might not have dared to bother Jews yet. The authorities also had more important things to do at the moment. Besides, they'd been bribed.

The peasants who came to the Green Market with wagons full of food thronged around the stand while the Nusens, Fryds, and Meinemers measured, bargained, shouted, and sweated. Izak and I would bring pots of food from the house and run out for lemonade. Belcia took care of the cooking. She got her fresh dairy products, poultry, and vegetables straight from the market, obtained by bartering with the peasants. For dinner, we'd have chopped liver with onions, soup with really yellow noodles made from plenty of eggs, hen's neck stuffed with flour and chicken fat, carrot *tsimmes,* and compote made from apples and plums. At those dinners we'd recall the cold and rainy nights when you had to steal up to a peasant's hut for a few potatoes cooked in their skins. Then Izak and I would be sent out for a few more bottles of the most expensive lemonade, and with the change we'd be allowed to buy ourselves ice cream or candy. After dinner, they'd throw a great mound of dirty, crumpled banknotes on the table and then stack them, count them, and divide them up.

In the last days of April people massed on Freedom Square, where the loudspeakers relayed communiqués from the front. Newspaper boys ran around the streets shouting "Berlin fell, Hitler's in hell!" The newspapers were snatched out of their hands.

There were grand parades of soldiers and youth, parade after parade—on the first of May, the third of May, the ninth of May.

People watched in silence as the troops filed by wearing ugly Russian puttees, shabby uniforms, the white eagle insignia of Poland but minus the crown. Everybody was enthusiastic, however, about the boy scouts, who marched in military style and wore brand new uniforms, colored scarves, and lilies in their caps.

"When did they manage to make all that for them?" wondered the Meinemers, Nusens, and Fryds.

"Where there's a will there's a way. . . . Don't you understand? Don't you see what's going on here?"

Fourteen-year-old boys wore thick spats and army leggings and had German bayonets strapped to their belts. Adults, with merit badges sewn on their sleeves, marched at the head of the scout troop. "Long live our scouts!" came shouts from the sidewalk. "Our future, our hope! The true Poland!"

Backs straight, the scouts marched in parade step, looking the people on the sidewalks straight in the eye, as if to say, "Yes, it's we who are your hope, your Poland, your only army."

They were followed by young people in civilian clothes carrying banners, some red and white, some red, some green. They marched down Piotrkowska Street, which had been called Hitler Street during the Occupation, to Freedom Square, which had been called Hitler Square. As they marched, they sang, "We're marching down Piotrkowska Street again, we'll strangle Hitler and his gang!" The people on the sidewalk repeated, "We'll strangle Hitler and his gang!" "From Piotrkowska we'll go to Sterling, to hang Goebbels and Göring!" the marchers continued, and everyone repeated, "To hang Goebbels and Göring!" "From Sterling we'll go to Berlin, to hang Hitler ugly as sin!" "To hang Hitler ugly as sin!" everybody shouted.

My mother and I, the Fryds, and the Nusens stood together on the street. "Thanks unto thee, O Lord our God, that thou has let us live and witness this day," Fryd said in Hebrew. Those were the words of an old Jewish prayer.

During these heady days Belcia Meinemer married a man whom Izak and I had stopped on the street and asked, "Amkhu?" At that time Jews were marrying quickly. Anyone they could. Widowers married widows, invalids married invalids. The blind married the lame and paralytics the tubercular. A man we knew in the building next door, an old hunchbacked bachelor, married a pretty young woman who had returned from Ravensbrück with a withered leg.

Everyone was in a hurry, afraid there wouldn't be enough partners to go around. And no one wanted to be left all alone. Every marriageable man was worth his weight in gold, and people weren't being choosy. Besides, not everyone was as young as Belcia. They had to hurry. Their best years were already long past. They had lost their children and weren't at all certain that God, who had not been much in evidence for a long time, would bless them with children again. But, if they couldn't count on having children, they could try to replace a father, mother, brother, or sister for one another. Marriage had never been so precious.

The wedding of Belcia and Moniek did not take place in front of the house, as custom dictated, but in the apartment. People did not yet have the courage to take their Jewish customs out into the street.

For a wedding canopy, a patterned German bedspread had been opened up in the dining room and was held up by four people, each taking a corner. Substituting for her dead parents, Belcia's brothers accompanied her to the canopy. The groom, Moniek, had no one at all, so Nusen and Fryd walked arm in arm with him. Then Moniek recited the prayer for his departed parents and all his nearest kin. It was not a happy ceremony. After Moniek said Kaddish, and the cantor, in a high tenor voice, asked God for mercy, people began crying, for nobody ever needed God's mercy as much as the Jews. And nobody else takes on as much responsibility when they marry as do Jews. So a Jewish wedding usually cannot be a happy event. Nobody has as many dead to lament as do the Jews, and certainly no one has had as many as they did in that May of 1945.

After the wedding, Belcia and Moniek came to live in the dining room, and so my mother had to find another place for us. There were no longer any apartments available on the better streets nor any furnished places like the ones where the Nusens, Fryds, and Meinemers were living. My mother found a room with a kitchen near the old Poznański factory. It was really a part of a larger apartment that had two entrances: one from the front, the other from the rear. The front part of the apartment, which had a balcony, was occupied by the Gaworczyk family. Though we were in back, we had the kitchen and the bathroom. There was neither a bathtub nor a stove for heating water in our bathroom, but at least we didn't have to go down to the courtyard to use the toilet and to get water. My mother was surprised that the Gaworczyks had taken the front part, which had no running water. After all, you have to do the wash, clean, and cook.

"I've gone out to get water my whole life," said Mrs. Gaworczyk. "And we've always lived in the rear where there's never been any sun. They say better times are coming for us workers, so let there be a little sun in the house, too."

Both Gaworczyks, father and son, worked at the Poznański factory. For us, the fact that they lived in the front was one of the apartment's advantages. All sorts of strangers came around to apartments and people didn't feel secure in their homes. Especially Jews. Besides, you had to know how to hold on to the apartment you had bought. A few days after we moved in, somebody who had paid the same soldier my mother had arrived and demanded we vacate the apartment. Fortunately, both Gaworczyks were home. They took the man by the arms and threw him out. My mother went immediately to the Housing Department to get an official allocation. They told her they didn't issue allocations to people who had moved in illegally, which meant they wanted a bribe, too. My mother went to see Comrade Jasinski, an older man who was the head of the Housing Department, and told him some of what we'd been through during the Occupation. She was given an official allocation, two copies. Jasinski told her to nail one up on the door and to hide the other one well.

As expected, the one on the door was torn off. But when the "new owner" came, this time with a policeman he had paid to accompany him, my mother got out her other copy with Jasinski's seal and signature and showed it to them. The man in the police uniform demanded that my mother hand him the copy, but my mother refused and only showed it to him from a distance. From then on we were left in peace.

Soon after that, Aron moved to Łódź with his wife and child. He was also accompanied by Adek, who came in from Mińsk Mazowiecki with his fiancée and her brother. Adek had not been able to find any of his family. His fiancée's brother, Stefek, was a couple of years older than I. Adek's fiancée, who was all of sixteen, had survived by living as a nun in a convent. The nuns were afraid of keeping Stefek, who was circumcised, and they gave him to partisans in the forest; only the leader knew Stefek was a Jew. Adek and his fiancée stayed with us while trying to get visas for France. This worked out well for my mother because she had started traveling to the West with Aron and didn't have anyone to leave me with.

People brought back kitchen utensils, tableware, bedclothes, bedspreads, towels, tablecloths, portable electric stoves, radios, and bicycles from the West. These things of value were obtained from Germans in exchange for flour, salted bacon, and cigarettes. And sometimes for nothing. People would simply go into houses and take what they wanted. If any help was needed, they'd ask the first soldier they saw and offer him a pack of cigarettes. The soldier would not only accompany them but, if necessary, force the door open with the butt of his rifle.

"Take whatever you want," the soldiers would say. "Take it without asking! Don't show them any mercy! It's not their stuff anyway! It's all been stolen!"

And in fact, not only were German items brought back from the West but French, Belgian, Dutch, and Czech things were as well. People just took what they wanted. "Anyway, it's still less than they should have coming," they'd say, emptying German bureaus and wardrobes. But my mother just couldn't do that and always gave something in exchange. Aron brought me compasses, whistles, and Finnish knives. And he talked with me.

"Remember how I brought you to Warsaw, all covered with lice from that dugout in the forest?" he asked. "Remember how we walked by the mill in broad daylight? A gendarme was standing on the bridge and a peasant with a wagon was waiting for his turn at the mill. You don't remember, but I remember how that peasant's eyes popped when he saw us. I knew him well. I used to sell him horses. One peep from him and that would have been the end of us. I took off my cap and I said, 'Praised be Jesus Christ.' Then I told you to take off your cap and bow to the gendarme. 'Make a nice little bow to the officer,' I said, and we kept on going as if it were nothing, without looking back even once, because we weren't supposed to. But how could we know what was going on behind us? The gendarme might have been watching us. Maybe he'd already aimed his rifle. How could I know what that peasant I used to sell horses to was going to do? There are all kinds of peasants. Maybe the horses I sold him weren't good enough. Two weeks later the Germans came upon the dugout where your grandfather, grandmother, both your aunts, and your little uncle were hiding. . . . And you wouldn't be here either if I hadn't taken you away when I did. I took you away just in time. Nobody else could have done it. They wouldn't have known where, when, how. Nobody would have wanted to run the risk. With a kid? . . . Nobody else would have done it. So tell me, would you like me to be your father?"

"Yes, I'd like that."

Aron wanted my mother and me to go to the West with him and stay there. Many people had gone to the West and not returned. Some men married German women there. Even Jews did that. There were a great many women there, almost nothing but women. Men would just walk into apartments, better than anything they'd ever dreamed of. Neatly dressed, well-mannered women offered them the clothes that had belonged to their husbands, fathers, brothers. They pressed their suits, cleaned their boots, washed their feet, just so they wouldn't go away and leave them all alone again. They'd say how lonely they'd been these last few years. And they were nicest to Jews! The young men were moved by all this. Especially those who had come from Russia, who had never seen such apartments and such women, and who didn't know all that the Germans had done to the Jews.

"But I was in Poland and I saw it all," said Aron. "So how could I marry a German woman?"

"What are you talking about, Aron? You've already got a wife and child!" replied my mother.

"But she's no wife for me. I married her because I had to, everybody knows that. What do I have in common with her? I'm not even sure whether the child's mine or not. Other guys slept with her, too. If I had known I was going to see you again. . . . You know I love your boy as if he were my own son. Didn't I save his life? And who do you think I did that for? For you."

"You can't leave a woman all alone with a child," my mother would reply. She thought that, if Aron could leave one woman with a child, then he could leave her, too, later on, especially if he met someone else, younger and without any children.

When my mother was home, Adek and his fiancée slept in the kitchen on a straw mattress. When my mother was away, they slept in her bed. Morning and night Stefek and I would hear a creaking sound from that end of the room. Adek's fiancée cooked for us and cleaned up. She went around the house in a very short nightgown—when my mother wasn't home, of course. When we sat at the table, Adek kept his hand on her thighs the whole time. They were more than just engaged. They thought of themselves as husband and wife and people treated them as such, but they hadn't married because single people could get their exit visas more quickly than families could.

Izak and I were always arguing with Stefek. He wore a big Polish army cap that fell over his ears and eyes; Izak Fryd wore a gray shirt with the six-pointed-star insignia of a Zionist youth organization, Shomer Hatzair; I wore Captain Gopin's epaulets; and we'd argue over who had really won the war. Izak and I always stood up for the Russian side, Stefek for the Americans and the English.

"If it hadn't been for America," he'd say, "it would have been all over for Russia! America sent Russia ammunition, canned goods, warm clothes and boots, everything they needed. What could the Russians have done without all that?"

"And what could the Americans have done with all their boots and canned food if it hadn't been for the Russians? Who would have done the fighting? The Russian soldiers were the best and bravest!"

"That's right," seconded Izak. "They'd drink a hundred grams of pure alcohol and go on the attack, not afraid of anything!"

"And afterward there'd be twice as many Russians killed as Germans," Stefek would reply.

"That's because sometimes they'd get a little too drunk."

"And because the NKVD was right behind them and anyone who moved too slow got shot."

"That's not true. The NKVD didn't have to force them on. They'd throw themselves with grenades under German tanks and hurl themselves onto machine guns. And Russian pilots wouldn't jump out of their burning planes, but crash them right onto the Germans, just to kill more of them!"

"Why did they hurl themselves onto machine guns? Wouldn't it have been better to use grenades? And why did they throw themselves under tanks? The Americans used tanks and airplanes against tanks. And why didn't the Russians jump out of their airplanes? . . . Because the NKVD executed anyone who lost a plane. The Americans told their soldiers, we can make a tank or an airplane in twenty hours but we had to wait twenty years for you, so don't worry about your airplane, just save yourself and come back. But for the Russians an ordinary rifle is more important than a man."

"It's no trick to win when you've got so many tanks and airplanes."

"And what kind of trick is it to send thousands of soldiers to their deaths? Until the Germans were out of ammunition. . . ."

"That's not the soldiers' fault. Sure the Germans or the Americans wouldn't have attacked like that, but the Russians did! . . . That's why they won!"

"Besides, Russia has the most people in the world," Izak observed. "If only Palestine had one-tenth as many. . . ."

"If it wasn't for the Russians," I said, "we wouldn't be here now."

"You're stupid!" replied Stefek. "You think they cared about you or me? If the Germans hadn't attacked Russia, Russia would have just stood by and watched the Germans killing Jews, Poles, and anybody else they felt like killing, without so much as lifting a finger."

Neither Izak nor I could take any more of this and would pounce on Stefek and start punching him.

Waiting for visas took a long time, and Adek came to the conclusion that he, too, could make a couple of profitable trips to the West in the meantime. My mother agreed that he go instead of her because she no longer felt comfortable traveling with Aron.

The trip there and back was supposed to take a week. But a week passed and Adek and Aron hadn't come back. Adek's fiancée began to get worried. My mother comforted her, telling her that the trains weren't running on schedule, and there was a shortage of coal, cars, and locomotives, which broke down often, delaying trains for an entire day.

But Adek's fiancée grew more worried all the time. It turned out she was pregnant. My mother told her to stop worrying because it could harm the child, but that didn't help. She stopped eating, couldn't sleep, never left the house. All she did was listen intently for footsteps on the stairs. Every one she heard she thought was Adek's. Finally, my mother went to the militia.

At that time trains were being stopped in the forests or just before they'd arrive at a station, at junctions, sometimes in open country. People were pulled out of the cars. Armed men examined papers, suitcases, faces. They dragged Communists and Jews away to the left. When my mother and Aron traveled to the West, they always took their forged ID *Kennkarten* from the time of the Occupation, and never told anyone they were Jews.

But Adek didn't have a *Kennkarte*. And maybe he looked Jewish. He did have a slight Yiddish accent. Adek thought these were ordinary bandits. He held out his sack to them. "That's all I've got, it's yours, take it!" But they weren't interested in his things. "Jew!" they said and shot him before he knew what was happening.

"What else do they want from us!" cried my mother. "You could understand it if they killed Communists, that's political. . . . But why Jews?"

"Hard to say," replied the investigating officer. "They've gotten used to killing Jews."

Aron wasn't on the train when Adek was returning home. He had stayed in the West. He sent us a postcard from Austria. He said that Austria was a beautiful country, he liked it there very much, and would probably get married soon.

Adek's former fiancée and Stefek joined a kibbutz group leaving for Palestine.

"Remember, don't despair," my mother said to her. "Despair doesn't do you any good; you might lose the child you're carrying, and that you mustn't do! Don't think about anything else. You're a woman— this is your greatest responsibility. And more important for you than for other women."

After a time a letter arrived from Cyprus. It turned out that Aron's Austrian marriage hadn't lasted very long either. Stefek and his sister ran into him on Cyprus in an English camp for Jews who had attempted to enter Palestine illegally. In the next letter we learned that Aron had married Adek's fiancée and become the father of Adek's son.

Uszer came to us near the end of the summer. My mother wasn't home. I was in bed with chicken pox and covered in scabs. Uszer was wearing an American army shirt and knee-length English shorts. He also had a German knapsack trimmed with horsehide. His face and legs were swollen.

"You don't know me," he said. "But I know your mother well. And I knew your grandfather from Dobre. The whole family. I know they're not alive. I was in Dobre. There's nobody left there. . . . I wasn't living in Dobre anymore when your mother got married, so there's no way you could know me. I used to live in Warsaw. On Złota Street. My older daughter would be about the same age as you. There's nobody left in Warsaw either. Your other grandfather, the one from Nowa Wieś, had a brother in Warsaw who lived on Złota too. I knew him. A cow dealer. He traveled as far as Holland. He got a passport for Argentina in 1939. He was rich, he could afford it. He wanted all of you to leave. Why didn't you?"

"I don't know."

"Yes, who could have known then? Didn't you have a sister or a brother?"

"I had a brother. He was very little."

"What happened to him?"

"When we were running away, my mother left him with some people, but someone informed and the Germans found him."

"I wonder if your mother has changed much."

"She's a blond now."

"A blond?"

"Yes, she dyed her hair."

"I got your address from Słoń in Mińsk Mazowiecki. I found out my brother Nusen was alive but nobody knew his address. All I got was yours. . . . You're reading this?" he asked, picking up the book that lay on my quilt. "*Konrad Wallenrod* by Adam Mickiewicz. . . . God, how long ago that was. . . . How old are you?"

"Nine."

"And you understand everything in the book?"

"I do. It's about a boy who was raised among the Teutonic Knights and who thought he'd be one of them when he grew up. But, before he grew up, he found out that he was a Lithuanian. And he also found out what the Teutonic Knights had done to his father and his brothers and his uncles and to all Lithuanian villages."

"And what's this?" he asked, picking up an album of drawings.

"Those are drawings from Treblinka. The naked women with their hands raised are dying and those thin lines falling onto their heads and winding around their necks, that's the gas. . . . And where were you before coming here?" I asked, looking at his swollen legs.

"Austria."

"They say it's a beautiful country."

"Yes, but I came from Mauthausen. . . ."

Uszer moved in with the Nusens, Fryds, and Meinemers and started helping them in their business. He came in very handy because he knew bookkeeping and how to deal with the bureaucracy. He was the best-educated and most able member of his family. When he was fourteen, his father, a shoemaker, had sent him to Warsaw to pick up orders and buy leather. Uszer was reading by then. His father never suspected he would bring Communist brochures as well as leather back from Warsaw.

After serving in the army, Uszer had gone straight to a prison for political offenders, where in four years he completed his education, learning not only political economy and the principles of revolution but history, geography, even mathematics. That prison held teachers and professors Uszer could never have dreamed of studying with otherwise. "Gentlemen, time for your French lesson," the guard would call, knocking on the cell door—they studied languages as well. They had all the books that had been forbidden them or had been too expensive when they were at liberty. They had their own party self-government and discipline. The packages they received from organizations aiding political prisoners were divided equally among them all. They also shared their packages from home in the same way. True equality and justice prevailed.

And there wasn't a trace of anti-Semitism. On the contrary, the Polish prisoners were particularly cordial to their Jewish comrades. Not only because there were more Jews than Poles both in the party and in prison. It was party principle that, after taking power in Poland, the Communists would put an end to anti-Semitism and all the sufferings of the Jews. Jewish workers and intellectuals would take part in the political and economic life of society and would enjoy equally the blessings of science and culture. Anti-Semitism and racism were considered nightmares that lay in the very nature of aggressive, capitalist society, racked by contradictions and ruled by the law of the jungle. Scientific Marxism, the basis of communism, proved—in a simple, ingenious manner accessible to all—that these contradictions would disappear when the means of production were socialized and the division between exploiters and exploited eliminated. Then there would be no struggle for existence, and persecution would disappear. It simply will no longer be in anyone's interest. People will be appreciated because of their value to society, not their social origin; the forces of production, hitherto restrained by the capitalist profit motive, will be liberated and produce so much that, when fairly divided, there will be more than enough for everyone. Conflicts between nations will also disappear. How could there be any conflict between nations in which communism had been established? There will be no more instances of one nation exploiting another or one state imposing its will on another. There will be no more wars, so typical of the capitalist world, for, where there are no conflicting interests, war is pure nonsense. Not only that, under communism, states will cease to exist altogether. Nations as well. They simply won't be needed anymore. Isn't that clear? Isn't that brilliantly simple?

Yes, it was simple, for Jewish shoemakers and tailors, doctors and professors. Communism was the best way out for Jews, if not the only way. It was their best refuge. In the party they were treated as equals, full-fledged members. They could develop themselves, dedicate themselves, display their talents.

At that time, the Polish Communists, whom no Polish woman would marry, began marrying their female Jewish comrades. This also proved them to be ideologically free of any bourgeois prejudices. But you hardly ever heard of any Polish woman marrying a Jewish Communist. Mostly because very few Polish women were Communists. The poorer a Polish woman was, the more often she went to church. And those who were better off had no reason to do anything as rash as marrying a man who was not only a Jew but a Communist. If they really wanted to aggravate someone, one or the other was quite enough. It was only after the war that Polish women started marrying Jewish Communists.

After getting out of prison, Uszer, as a Communist and convicted criminal, had no reason to return to Dobre. He stayed in Warsaw, without a steady job, and not only Polish women but Jewish women as well were in no hurry to marry him. Finally, one of his relatives, who were afraid that Uszer would get in more trouble and bring still greater disgrace on the family, took him on as a salesman in his shop. Uszer proved very conscientious, hard working, capable. He established credit, married, and set himself up in a small grocery store on Złota Street. He was thrifty, didn't drink or smoke, and started doing quite well for himself. He lost his faith in politics when his professors from Wronki prison, who went to Russia in exchange for Poles being held in Soviet prisons, were shot in Moscow as "traitors" and "provocateurs" just as Communist Russia was signing a pact with the Nazis.

In the ghetto, Uszer belonged to an underground organization that made use of his former connections with Polish Communists in order to get weapons. They had to pay dearly for every rusty old pistol and defective grenade detonator. "The party needs money," said the Communists. And the underground group should have been grateful— the Communists could have taken the money and not sent anything, and what could you have done to them? These were people who were guided only by their "lofty goal" and the principle that in pursuing that goal they need take nothing else into account. And, when they realized it was not their people running the ghetto's fighting group, they did in fact take the money and send no arms.

Uszer had a supply of flour, kasha, and beans hidden in the ghetto, so his children didn't die of hunger. By the time he was deported in the fall of '42, he had managed to get his elder daughter, with a goodly sum of money, out of the ghetto. The younger child, still breast-feeding, went with its mother to Treblinka.

In Treblinka the women and children were sent off to the left side. The old and the sick as well. Of those remaining, the Germans began selecting expert metalworkers. Uszer said he was a lathe operator. It turned out that he had made the right choice, since in the end only the lathe operators, locksmiths, and tinsmiths remained on the right side.

Of course, anyone could have seen at once that Uszer was no lathe operator, but he was quick to learn and tried hard. The foreman, a German, knew what such qualities were worth and gave him helpful hints.

Uszer stole empty cement bags. He made a hole in the bottom of the bag for his head and two holes in the sides for his arms. This vest, hidden under his striped jacket, protected him from the wind. When his legs started to swell up, he rubbed them with machine oil and bandaged them with strips torn from a blanket. In a field or on a road, he kept his eyes on the ground and never overlooked an apple core, carrot, or beet. If an SS man noticed, Uszer would cover his head with his hands and fall to his knees covered in blood from the blows, but nobody ever took what he'd found away from him. And he was never afraid of grabbing the next apple core. He also collected cigarette butts. But not to smoke. He sold them. For a spoonful of soup or a piece of bread. "If Hitler doesn't finish you off, we'll do it ourselves!" shouted the anti-Semites, who were helpless against Uszer and the other Jews who didn't smoke.

During the final winter, the oil didn't help anymore. Abscesses started appearing on the swellings. The Kapo came every morning to Uszer's plank and waited to see if he could get up or not. If somebody couldn't get up, or even if he could but was unable to drag himself to roll call, the Kapo would take him under the arms and drag him over to a barrel of water, where he would be submerged to determine if he was still fit to live. His head would be submerged. An SS man would hold him under. Always a little too long.

The hardest thing to endure was the *Entlausung,* the delousing. The prisoners' clothes were removed for disinfection, and meanwhile they had to stand outside, naked in the freezing cold, and wait. Many died there. Uszer collapsed during the final *Entlausung.* When the order was given for the prisoners to return to the barracks, the Kapo grabbed Uszer under the arms, but instead of to the water barrel, he dragged him to his plank bed. There, before everyone's eyes, he covered Uszer with a blanket, then brought him a bowl of hot soup and said, "Take it, Jew, eat it! Just remember it was me who brought you this soup. . . ."

"Could I have ever dreamed of eating at a table like this again," Uszer said at a Sunday breakfast as my mother served herring in oil, cottage cheese with radishes, eggs fried with onions, and challah, apple pie, and cheesecake she had made herself.

When Uszer married my mother, the cantor himself said Kaddish, since Uszer didn't know such things. All Uszer said was "Amen." I stood under the canopy, between Uszer and my mother. Everyone cried as if it were a funeral, not a wedding. That's how people treated a marriage between a widow and widower who hadn't been able to hold a funeral for those with whom they'd once, and some quite recently, stood under the canopy. Watching the ceremony, people were horrified by how quickly and how much everything can change. And the thought that once again they were starting out from scratch filled them with fear.

There were tears whenever Jews assembled. The more Jews, the more tears. Every Sunday Uszer took us to morning concerts, where a few Jewish performers, mostly amateurs, sang prewar Jewish songs. It didn't matter whether the songs were sad or happy, people cried.

But at no other time did things ever reach the extremes they did one Sunday morning when, instead of a concert, they showed a prewar Jewish film *The Town of Belz.* It's hard to say how many Jews were in Łódź at that time. Seven hundred and seventy had survived in the ghetto. Maybe a few hundred more had returned from the concentration camps. A few hundred had arrived with the Polish-Russian army. There were also some two thousand survivors from other cities and towns, people like us. And all of them wanted to get into the hall, which could not hold more than five hundred people. They broke the doors, all the mirrors, railings, and windows. The tickets, bought at black market prices, meant nothing now since nobody could check them. The throng pressed from every side and through every possible entrance. My mother never even made it into the lobby. Uszer pushed me in front of him. The lobby was so packed I couldn't breathe. I started shouting, "Let me out, I'm suffocating!" Women shouted, too. But nothing could be done, there was no way to get out. People tried to remove the women who had fainted by passing them over their heads. Uszer managed to lift me up and seat me on his shoulders and this way walked me inside, where three or four people seemed to be on every chair. All the space around the walls and between the rows was filled. There was so little air, as if there were some invisible throng hovering above our heads. The lights went out and, for a moment, complete silence reigned. But, when the well-known song came on—"Oh Belz, my beloved Belz, my little *shtetele* where all of my family . . ."—terrible cries burst from everyone. Not weeping, not wailing, but a great collective groan and cry of pain. As if a mass execution had taken place. You couldn't hear the words of the song or the melody. You couldn't even see the screen because everyone had risen, standing on tiptoe to see. But at the same time, people covered their eyes and faces with their hands. This went on until the film was over.

The money the Nusens, Fryds, and Meinemers made at the market wasn't hidden in mattresses or deposited in any bank. With that money they bought American dollars, which they set aside for passports, visas, and tickets. Neither they nor Uszer and my mother wanted to stay in Poland. They didn't want to be constantly encountering traces of the dead and to have the memory of what they'd endured constantly before their eyes. Besides, they had no more courage. Who could guarantee them that after a while it wouldn't all happen again? If something like that could happen once, all the more reason it could happen again. Once the way has been shown, any fool can do it the second time. And that was what they feared most.

Dollars were expensive, a thousand zlotys each. And, since passports and visas weren't entirely legal, you had to pay a high price for them. And what about travel expenses? You also needed a little money to live on, at least for a while, in those distant foreign lands where we knew no one and no one knew us and where, perhaps, nobody even wanted to know us. People were very afraid. So everyone tried to save as much money as possible and to buy as many dollars as possible.

The better merchandise from the factories also had to be paid for in dollars because the manufacturers needed dollars, too. But it was worth it because with your dollars you could buy merchandise that could be sold more quickly and at a higher profit, which could be used to buy even more dollars. People who had inherited property had it easiest. They would sell it and leave, especially in big cities, where no one was afraid to go and reclaim what they owned. People who had nothing and saw no chance of making any money were also leaving. They would pack up a knapsack and wend their way through Czechoslovakia, Germany, and Austria. Of the two evils, they preferred to be poor there rather than here. People like us, the Nusens, Meinemers, and Fryds stayed the longest. In the meantime, Polish money began losing its value. Dollars grew more expensive but it was against the law to raise prices. Inspectors began coming around, and extortionists. It was hard to tell one from the other.

One day we went from the market to the Nusens' for dinner. As usual, after the meal the money was poured out onto the table. Suddenly, the doorbell rang. I was playing checkers with Izak in the kitchen. When I heard the bell, I ran and opened the door. Two men in gabardine coats stood in the doorway. "Are your mommy and daddy at home?" "Everybody's home," I said. "Please come in."

Nothing happened to anyone; they just took the money and left, though Nusen did give me a smack in the face. We never found out who those men really were. But they took more than was on the table, and our departure had to be put off quite some time. Since Belcia and Mrs. Fryd were pregnant, they began wondering whether it wouldn't be better to give birth here, where at least you knew you had a roof over your head and enough to eat. Then, to everyone's surprise, it turned out that Frymka was also pregnant. She was older than her husband, forty-six.

My mother wasn't pregnant, but Uszer let everyone know he wasn't leaving until he had made every effort to locate his daughter, whom at one point he had given to a woman outside the ghetto. He finally found the woman but the child was not with her. She said she'd given the child to the nuns in an orphanage. Uszer demanded she go there with him. However, the child wasn't in that convent, and the nuns maintained that there had never been a Jewish child there.

"What do you mean, never?" the woman argued. "I left her here myself. Perhaps she had been transferred. . . ."

The nuns directed them to another convent, where there was supposed to be a Jewish child. But the woman didn't want to go, saying she had a lot of work at home. Uszer promised to pay her for the time she'd lose. When she continued to refuse, he threatened to have her investigated. The woman agreed and went with him.

But the girl in the other convent didn't look like Uszer's daughter. She was older and her hair was completely different.

"A child's hair can change," persuaded the woman to whom Uszer had entrusted his daughter.

"But this one's older," Uszer objected.

"How do you know she's older? She hasn't got a birth certificate. They just wrote anything down. A year more for one, a year less for another."

But Uszer insisted they go to one more convent.

"You don't know what you want yourself. Whoever heard of anyone being so choosy about children."

At the third orphanage, Uszer was shown a girl who was the right age and had hair like his daughter. The nuns said she was a Jewish child from Warsaw. This time the woman accompanying Uszer was absolutely certain he had found his daughter.

"You were right to insist on coming here. It's divine providence, it's fate. It was your heart telling you what to do. . . . One look is enough to see how much she resembles you."

"Do you recognize me?" asked Uszer.

"No," the little girl said.

"Do you remember your mommy?"

"No, I don't."

Uszer touched her hair.

"You don't remember your mother's hair? Was it blond or brown? Tell me."

"I don't know."

"Do you remember if you had a little sister, much smaller than you?"

"I don't remember," the little girl said, lowering her head.

"Her hair is just like my wife's," said Uszer. He opened up a bag of cookies and candies. "Would you like to leave here with me?"

"Yes," the little girl said. She was pale and had a large, protruding stomach. In the orphanage they fed her soup three times a day.

Frymka clutched her head when Uszer brought the girl home.

"What have you done?" she cried. "That's not your child! Are you blind? Can't you see? I remember what your daughter looked like. She doesn't look like you or your wife either. Give her back! You already have one child that's not your own. You need another one?" Frymka was always opposed to Uszer's marrying my mother. "Go give her back. She doesn't even look like a Jewish child. Just look at those bulging eyes."

"It's her good luck she doesn't look Jewish," said Uszer. "Otherwise, she wouldn't be here. . . . Ania, do you want to go back to the orphanage?"

"No, I don't!" cried the girl.

"I won't give her back to the orphanage," said my mother. "It doesn't matter whose child she is. She's staying with us."

Uszer bought Ania a German bed with a screen on each side that could be raised and lowered. When we went to sleep, Uszer would sit on her bed and ask her to "fuss with Daddy." Ania would put her hand on his head and run her fingers though his thin, graying hair.

"You see, she knows exactly what 'fuss with Daddy' means. She remembers! She really is my daughter. Mine and no one else's!"

My mother, who had always wanted a daughter, made dresses for Ania out of her old clothes, braided her hair, and pinned a different bow in it every day. I was happy, too, because I had always wanted a sister. Izak and the other boys envied me. None of the other Jewish children we played with had a sister or a brother.

One day the telephone rang. Uszer was at the market with the Nusens, the Fryds, and the Meinemers. My mother answered the phone.

"Did you people take a child from an orphanage?"

"Yes."

"Can we come see you?"

"Who is speaking?"

"We're looking for a child, too."

"But what does that have to do with us?"

"We'd like to see the girl."

"But what for?"

"Just to see her."

"Impossible."

"Why?"

"She's not at home."

"We'll come when she is."

"She's not living here."

"What? Where is she then? Didn't your husband take her from the orphanage?"

"True. But then we sent her away."

"Where? She's not in the orphanage."

"We sent her to the mountains."

"Where in the mountains?"

"I don't know."

"What do you mean you don't know? Who does then?"

"My husband."

"May I speak to him?"

"He's not at home."

"When will he be home?"

"I don't know. Please stop questioning me! I don't even know whom I'm talking to," said my mother, hanging up.

My mother didn't tell Uszer anything. Whenever the phone rang she'd run to answer it first, saying, "Wrong number." Finally, for some reason, the phone went out of order, and meanwhile, my mother managed to get the Jewish Committee to send me and Ania away from the foul, smoky city because we were weak from the wartime malnutrition and our health was in jeopardy. We were sent to Helenówek near Łódź, to a Jewish Children's Home founded before the war by

Chaim Rumkowski, who later on became the chairman of the Łódź ghetto. While we were in Helenówek, my mother kept trying to get passports and visas so we could all leave the country.

The Children's Home was supported by the Joint Distribution Committee, and we were better off there than we had been at home with my mother and Uszer. We were given American condensed milk, American ground sardines, American powdered eggs, canned peach compote, and thick American chocolate bars. We wore checkered American coats, checkered shirts, checkered caps, checkered socks, and bright checkered scarves. We slept under green blankets with "U.S." written on them. The older boys would lock themselves in the boys' room and smoke dizzying American cigarettes, which they'd get from the men who guarded the Home. We also had American notebooks with rustling, incredibly white pages, clear plastic pencil boxes, and long colored pencils. We brushed our teeth with American toothbrushes and had an American Ping-Pong table and croquet set.

We were also well protected. The whole area was enclosed by a high, wire fence, and there was a guard booth by the gate. The guard was armed. After the pogrom in Kielce, two armed guards were stationed at the entrance, and at night some of the older boys stood watch with them.

Neither Ania nor I knew anything about sports or games, but the fact that we were brother and sister impressed the other children. Uszer and my mother visited us every Sunday. We would hold their hands tightly as we strolled together and showed everybody the candy they had brought us. It wasn't any better than the American candy we were all given, but we were the envy of everyone because few children were visited on Sundays.

People also came to Helenówek to look for their lost children, but they never found them there. There was great joy if a child was found by an aunt, uncle, or a distant cousin or even someone who had known his or her parents. Then the little group of us who ran out on Sundays to meet our visitors and to walk holding some grownup's hand would be increased by one more child. Ania and I liked it in Helenówek, and everybody liked us. With the possible exception of our director, Mrs. Rotholz.

We were certain that no intruder could ever enter our world. We could count on the guards for that. But it was a different story if someone wanted to run away. No one was ever caught running away. When we woke up in the morning, we'd see a neatly made bed, and one of us would be gone. That meant some adopted relatives had convinced him to run away. Some mornings we'd see two or three neatly made beds if a few boys ran away together. They always left their beds neatly made, with hospital corners. That was the style.

If two or three boys ran away together, that meant they'd run off to join a group leaving for Palestine. This infuriated Mrs. Rotholz. She'd call the militia, the Jewish Committee, the party. All for nothing, since by then the group would be long gone. The guards would shrug. They had no idea how the boys had done it. Over the fence, under the fence, through the fence. . . . Mrs. Rotholz threatened to fire them, but the guards laughed at this. They were single men without families or homes. They lived with us, watched over us day and night. They never got drunk and were truly devoted to us. Where would Mrs. Rotholz find other men like that?

They had lived for many years with gun in hand and knew their job well. Natek had fought in the Spanish Civil War. Then, unable to return to Poland, he went to Russia and entered Poland with the Russian army as a sergeant. Danek had served in the Polish army of General Anders. He had been in Palestine and had now returned from England to look for his family. Gerszon had been with partisans. We used to go to the guard booth, where they'd tell us stories: Natek about Spain, Danek about Palestine and Arab customs, Gerszon about mushrooms, berries, and plants that could be eaten or had medicinal properties. They never spoke of war. They didn't want to.

"You'd have to tell too much," they'd say.

"And what about the partisans?" we'd ask Gerszon. "What was that like?"

"The usual—cold, hunger, and lice," Gerszon would answer. "And, on top of that, everyone afraid of everyone else. . . . A nasty business!"

It was inevitable that Mr. and Mrs. Jarząbek, whom my mother had not given a chance to see Ania in Łódź, would show up in Helenówek. They came during the week, not on Sunday, when my mother, Uszer, and all the other visitors would be there. Mrs. Rotholz summoned

Ania and told her to wash up and change her clothes because someone had come to see her. I wanted to change my clothes, too, and go
with Ania because I thought anyone coming to see Ania was coming
to see me as well. But Mrs. Rotholz said the visitor only wished to
see Ania. This bothered me greatly and made me feel like I wasn't
Ania's brother anymore. I stood in the hall watching the door to Mrs.
Rotholz's office. When it opened, Ania walked out with a tall man
wearing glasses and two elegant ladies. The tall man was holding
Ania's hand, and she had a large chocolate bar in her other hand. One
of the ladies straightened the bow in Ania's hair. Ania blushed when
she saw me. I started following them, but Mrs. Rotholz glanced
sternly at me, and I had to stop.

Uszer and my mother went to a lawyer at once. What proof did
Mr. Jarząbek have that she was his child? None whatsoever. After all
that had happened, how could anyone have proof of anything? After
all we'd been through, you couldn't even be sure you yourself were
the same person you used to be. Everyone and everything had been
lost, your entire past. And now, when a man had miraculously recovered a part of what he had lost, how could anyone have the audac-
ity to come to take it away from him? How could they? Didn't they
have a heart, a Jewish heart? You had to be a barbarian to do something like that. People were trying to help each other as much as they
could. By joining together, starting families from what was left of
their lives and their courage. . . . So how could they do it? Let's say
we couldn't be certain the child was ours. But we'd come to love her,
and she'd become ours. Weren't there enough other orphans? It had
to be this one?

"It's King Solomon's court," said the lawyer. "If the judge isn't
completely certain who the real father is, we'll win the case."

After the first hearing, when the case was postponed until both
parties could present more convincing evidence, the advantage was
clearly on our side. However, Ania was to remain in Helenówek,
where both parties had the right to visit her. "Didn't I tell you there'd
be trouble!" said Frymka.

At the second hearing, Mr. Jarząbek, his sister, and his second
wife—his first wife, the mother of his child, had perished in Treblinka, as had Uszer's first wife—brought not only the woman to
whom Mr. Jarząbek had originally given his daughter for safekeeping

but the nun to whom that woman had later given the child. It turned out that the nun had kept the girl's birth certificate and brought it with her. The name on the birth certificate was Jarząbek. The nun stated that she recognized the woman whom Mr. Jarząbek had brought as the person who had given her the Jewish girl and birth certificate. The woman to whom Uszer had entrusted his child did not appear in court at all.

Uszer beseeched the judge for one more hearing. The judge explained that, either way, Uszer had the right to appeal the decision, which could be done by his attorney in the next few days. And so, although he understood Uszer's motives and sincerely sympathized with him, the judge saw no reason for a postponement.

Uszer was unable to present any additional hard evidence. The woman who had supposedly given his child to the convent had disappeared and could not be found at her previous address. The lawyer said quite frankly that, in these circumstances, he saw no chance of winning the appeal. He advised Uszer to withdraw, accept the verdict, and save himself time, money, and, most important, heartache.

But Uszer would not allow himself to be convinced. The Fryds, the Meinemers, and Frymka and Nusen as well came to the appeal hearing. Frymka took the witness stand and declared categorically that she remembered the girl perfectly and recognized her as Uszer's daughter. In his summation the lawyer traced the forty years of Uszer's life, forty years of calamity, as he put it. Finally, losing control of his voice, he cried, "Your Honor, here is a man who does not want to learn for a second time that his child is dead!"

The case continued for almost six months. In that time the visas and passports my mother had obtained expired, and she had to start all over again.

In the spring of that year, Fryd's sister Ryvka returned from Russia with a man she'd married there and their two young children. She came back in a contingent of Polish Jews who had been permitted to return from Central Asia, Siberia, and the Autonomous Republic of Komi. These were the Jews who had fled to the Soviet zone in 1939 or who had been exiled by the Russians themselves when they took eastern Poland.

At that time, Fryd's sister Ryvka and the other Polish Jews who found themselves in Russia were so horrified by what they saw there that they began to regret having fled from the Germans. Noticing this, the Soviet authorities good-naturedly announced that, if they were so eager to return home, they could. All they had to do was sign up.

The naive Polish Jews, who were very clever at getting along in their little Polish towns, had no feeling for real politics. What could the Germans do to us? they thought. Germans don't like the Jews? But weren't Jews used to not being liked? Germans shout, threaten, and intimidate because that's their policy, but, after all, they're a civilized nation. Let's say they'll even harass and persecute Jews. But when weren't the Jews harassed and persecuted? Sometimes more, sometimes less, but it always happened. And somehow the Jews always managed. Somehow they would this time, too. What mattered was that tormentors come and go, but the Jews remain. And what could the Russian *katsaps* do to them for wanting to return home? . . . So, they ran to sign up.

The *katsaps* ordered them to come to the cargo trains. They loaded them on and shut up the cars. A guard was posted on each car, and off they went. But not west—east.

"Where are you taking us?" asked the Jews. "Poland's to the west, not the east."

"Don't worry, brother," the Russian guards would answer good-naturedly. "If you were supposed to go west, you'd have gone west, but since you're going east, that means you're supposed to go east. The Soviet government knows the way."

There were Jews who knew the Soviets better, said Ryvka. They said nothing about wanting to return home. On the contrary, they declared that they desired nothing more than to become Soviet citizens. They were allowed to remain in Białystok; Minsk, Belarus; Vilna. From there the "shrewder" ones crossed back to Poland through the forest near Łomża and the river Bug. Unnecessarily because, less than two years later, the Germans came to Vilna and Lvov and swept up everyone anyway. Only some Jews who were on the eastern side of the river Dnieper and in southern Ukraine were evacuated with the factories and collective farms where they worked.

Ryvka's Russian husband had never seen pajamas before. Ryvka said that, when they first met, he used to brag that before the war he was rich because he owned a blue suit. She told us that once a Russian had taken her aside, made sure no one could overhear them, and asked if it were true that in the West, in Poland, you could just walk into a store and buy yourself a pair of shoes, the kind you wanted, or even two pairs if you wished? . . .

"It's not because of the war," said Ryvka. "They just didn't know any other life."

But, deep down, we envied Ryvka and those naive Jews who were deported to the taiga, the tundra, the polar bears. They felled timber, tilled hard earth, and were devoured by hunger, typhus, and lice, but they came back. A hundred thousand returned. But the "shrewd" ones who had crossed the Bug back into Poland and those who never left Poland vanished without a trace.

Contingents from the Soviet Union also came to Helenówek. Entire Children's Homes from Tashkent and Samarkand. American army cots were set up in the playrooms, the corridors, even in the attics; tents were pitched on the lawns. Not everyone was allowed to leave Russia, but no children were detained. Their fathers had been sent off to war and had not returned or had perished in other circumstances. If their mothers hadn't perished from hunger or disease, they remained in labor camps. The mothers who returned in separate contingents would come to Helenówek to find their children but would not take them away. Where would their children be better off than in Helenówek? It was just the other way around; the mothers would stay on at Helenówek, taking jobs in the kitchen or doing laundry and housekeeping.

The children, the girls as well as the boys, arrived from Russia with their heads shaved, but still lice began appearing. There were enough beds at Helenówek but too few washrooms and too little water. An epidemic of mange broke out, and special tents were set up for those ill with it. Along with the mange and lice came a rash of thefts.

Canned food, condensed milk, chocolate, and sausage were stolen. It seemed strange to us because no one ever went hungry in Helenówek. There may have been food shortages in other Children's Homes and orphanages, but not in ours, which was maintained by the Joint Distribution Committee, the UNRRA, and private persons in America and Switzerland—no great problem for them, since there were significantly fewer of us Jewish children in Poland than there were rich Jews in America and Switzerland.

The boys from Russia had enough to eat by day, so they ate their stolen food at night; what they couldn't eat they hid in their mattresses. They scorned any of us who didn't know how to steal or were afraid to. Mrs. Rotholz marshaled all forces in the struggle to restore respect for common property. The greater our common wealth, she'd tell us at assembly, the richer each of us is. So why steal? Stealing what belonged to us all was like stealing from yourself. Her speech seemed simple and logical, but somehow it was not quite convincing.

We had more faith in Miss Maria, who had come with the children from Russia. She was tall, thin, slightly stooped—her sparse hair was tied in an ugly bunch. She always wore the same dark gray dress, which made her look like a nun, and steel-rimmed spectacles that didn't much help her badly crossed eyes. Holding a book up close to her right eye, then to her left, she would read us Makarenko's book *Pedagogical Poem*. She translated directly into Polish from the Russian, which won our respect. The message of the book was that it's not the individual who is important but the collective, and the most contemptible things are selfishness, egotism, and private property.

We listened with great feeling to this story of homeless Russian children, depraved by civil war and hunger, whom the collective and the Soviet system had nevertheless brought up to be good people. We truly respected the ugly but wise Miss Maria, who knew several languages. She was also respected by the kids from Russia, who knew her better. They knew she wouldn't lie to us and that, unlike the others, she really believed in what she said.

But all this did not mean in the least that the raids on the storeroom came to a halt. The only difference was that now contemptible private property like the teachers' watches and money also began to be stolen. The thefts were done collectively. One or two boys would stand guard and in case of danger would shout "Cheese it!" If they were chased, the fastest and most agile boy would come out in the open so as to be the one pursued, while his buddies, loaded down with loot, could get away. No one who was caught would ever squeal. Russian boys never did things like that. In return, his friends would save him the biggest portion of condensed milk, sausage, and chocolate.

It wasn't individuals who were stealing but a collective, and so it wasn't a fair fight. It wasn't easy to resist Miss Maria's influence, but it was even harder to resist the collective, especially since Miss Maria herself had taught us about its strength and superior authority. The upshot was that even the non-Russian boys started stealing.

One evening, one of the boys, Lovka, informed us that the cucumbers and tomatoes in the greenhouse were now ripe. We removed a pane from the glass roof and lowered ourselves down silently. Crawling on all fours among the intoxicatingly fragrant plants beneath the glass roof, through which the whole star-strewn night sky could be seen, panting with excitement and delight, we moved forward, blindly sticking whatever we could grab inside our shirts. After some time, we were so weighted down and distended that we couldn't fit back through the opening we'd come in through and so had to throw back part of our loot. Back on the roof, I was about to replace the pane we'd removed when suddenly my hands shook, and the pane slipped and fell with a terrible crash. "Cheese it!" shouted Lovka. We ran behind the main building and hid in the basement heating room. We stayed there for half an hour eating bitter cucumbers and sour, half-green tomatoes. Then, one by one, we ran out and slipped back through the windows into our dormitory, where the lights had long since been turned off. Miss Maria was sitting in the dark on my bed.

"How could you do it?" she said. "You of all people. They steal because they always have. Since they were old enough to walk. They had to. . . . They learned how and now they can't break the habit. But you? You're different. So why? I thought you were different. . . . You've given me a great disappointment, Son."

"Son"—that was the word she used. Something caught in my throat when she said it and I couldn't utter a single word. I couldn't even cry. To this day, I can still feel that pain in my throat when I think of her. Soon afterward, Miss Maria left the Children's Home. She started working at the Polytechnic School in Warsaw as an instructor in Marxism-Leninism, which she believed in. Maybe the students there believed her just as we had. So it must have been terrible for her when a few years later everything she had taught turned out to be lies, hypocrisy, and cynicism. And the students blamed her for it. One night she came home from a meeting and turned on the gas. She alone. Those who were really to blame didn't turn on the gas.

After the stealing incident my mother took me back home from Helenówek.

The situation was growing worse in Łódź. Even small workshops were being taken away from their owners. The smallest ones, operating just a couple of looms, were crushed by surtaxes, and people simply gave them away. Anyone who dared to, installed a loom in a cellar or an attic. Others abandoned everything and left the country. Fryd's sister Ryvka left for America. Her husband was entitled to an American visa by the Russian quota, which hadn't been used for close to thirty years.

Now, however, Uszer began to vacillate.

"How can I go? What have I got? Do I have a profession? A real education? I don't even know the language over there. And I'm not young or strong enough for manual labor."

"And just what are you going to do for a living here?" my mother asked. "You're afraid to leave, but how are you going to make a living here? Forget everything else, how are you going to make a living?"

"I could get a job."

"A job? . . . Just look at the people with jobs. They live on bread with lard, ersatz coffee, and water soup, and their children go around barefoot!"

"That'll change. Don't you see, the country is being rebuilt? That takes time. They need people! People who would know how to organize production, who understand economics. . . . They need people for management and to run the cooperatives. You need a good head to get a cooperative going. And there's money to be made there, too. I could get a job like that."

"I don't want to hear about it," my mother said.

"You should see who is making careers for themselves today! Phonies, ignorant fools. . . ."

"And you'd like to stay here and spend the rest of your life with them?"

"They join the party and get any job they like. Now they're joining. . . . I joined when it didn't do you any good. You think I couldn't get such a job? All I'd have to do is show up. Lolek Kasman from Mińsk Mazowiecki is on the Central Committee. Lolek! All I'd have to do is call him up. I was his best student in Wronki."

"Don't you dare, you hear me? I'm not staying here. Stay here alone if you want to! I'll take my son and leave! You know I'm capable of it. . . ."

"What are you so afraid of? Anti-Semitism? There are anti-Semites everywhere. I understand, all the blood and terrible memories. . . . But where can you run to from that?"

"But don't you see what's happening here?"

"And what is happening here? Communism! Is that what you're afraid of? That's what all the Jews are afraid of. Not bad memories, not anti-Semitism. It's purely a class question and that's all it is!"

Uszer grew heated when stirred by ideas from his youth. He wasn't concerned with putting those ideas into practice. To speak of them was enough for him. To make his point. To be right. It made him feel young again and that sufficed.

"Backward, ignorant Jews!" he'd say. "They only listen to what the Jewish bourgeoisie says! They don't understand that only a Communist system can give them true equality! Jews are even favored now. . . . All the Communists have Jewish wives now and an open door to a career! Everyone in the government. . . ."

"The time will come when they'll divorce them. One look should tell you who you're dealing with. Could there be anything worse than a Polish Communist?"

"Don't say that, I knew several Polish Communists who were decent people."

"Now they need Jews! And how long will they need them? A year? Two years? Ten? And then what? When they don't need you anymore? Where will you go then? But that's not all. Who do you think will get it as soon as something goes wrong? The Jews! . . . And your friends, who need you so badly now, the ones sucking up to the Jews the most now, they'll be the first to turn. And they'll be the worst ones, too! You'll see, mark my words! As soon as something goes wrong, and it's bound to sooner or later. I don't want to hear another word on the subject."

Since goods at the market were becoming illegal, prices rose. For that reason, the peasants bringing in food also demanded higher prices, and, when they began to be punished for it, they stopped coming in altogether. Only the peddlers took the risk. They'd go to the countryside and buy up meat, poultry, and dairy products, but they demanded even higher prices. What you got from your ration card was never enough, and meanwhile wages stayed low. A strike broke out at the Poznański factory. The army and the UB, the security police, were sent in at once. Many people were arrested and beaten in the cellars on Anstadt Street, where the Gestapo had been housed during the Occupation. "So you felt like going on strike?!" the UB men shouted. "Against your own workers' government? There's insolence for you. . . ." The screams of the beaten men could be heard every night. The strike committee and anyone who had stood up were sent to Russia and never heard of again.

The arrests continued long after the strike. Both Gaworczyks, our neighbors, were taken in. They released the father but kept the son. A few weeks later a medical certificate arrived, stating that because of a chill he'd caught during the strike he developed pneumonia and was taken to a hospital, where he died.

The Gaworczyks had four sons. The oldest one went to war in 1939 and was killed. The second was deported by the Germans to do forced labor and never returned. The third was arrested by the Gestapo. He was held on Anstadt Street and then at Radogoszcz. The night before the Russians arrived, the Germans poured gasoline on the Radogoszcz prison and all the prisoners were burned alive.

When the news of his last son's death arrived, old Gaworczyk stopped going to work. He took to his bed and stayed there until he died. Mrs. Gaworczyk was taken to a mental institution because each day she would bring lunch to the factory for her husband and son, and at night she would walk up and down the stairs, knocking on every door and asking if any of her sons were there.

Belcia gave birth to a son. Everyone was delighted, but the question arose whether the child should be circumcised or not. Uszer, my mother, and the Nusens were absolutely opposed. So many children had perished because they were circumcised. Uszer considered circumcision a superstition. The Fryds expressed no opinion, but even the Meinemers, Belcia's brothers, advised against it. Moniek, Belcia's husband, couldn't make up his mind. To everyone's surprise, especially the women's, Belcia insisted on circumcision. "My child is not going to be afraid of being a Jew," she said. A little later, without a word to anyone, Belcia and Moniek obtained visas and without delay left for Palestine.

Uszer stopped talking about joining the party and remaining in Poland. My mother was buying things because HIAS, the Hebrew Immigrant Aid Society, was supposed to issue us papers for Venezuela. She ordered new pillowcases, sheets, shirts, and pajamas so that, when we were in Venezuela, we wouldn't have to buy anything there. We expected to leave that autumn. But it didn't turn out that way.

Rosenberg, an old friend of Uszer's from Wronki who had returned from Russia, showed up at our place one day. A meeting like this had to be celebrated. Uszer sent me for vodka, and my mother put everything she had on the table.

"You're living well," said Rosenberg, taking in the apartment.

In Russia, Rosenberg had never acknowledged that he had been a Communist in Poland before the war. The NKVD took a very dim view of Polish Communists. Many were arrested right away. They were beaten and forced to give the names of the activists who had come out against the Soviet pact with the Germans. Anyone who named names was sent to the North; anyone who refused was executed as a "traitor," "provocateur," or "foreign agent." There were those who said nothing. Some people wouldn't, but most could not stand the beatings and gave them whatever names they knew.

Rosenberg lived rather well there. "To live with a milkmaid is very good luck—there's milk to drink and the milkmaid to . . . ," he sang. Rosenberg had lived with a milkmaid in Russia.

One time the other women there wanted to see just what circumcision looked like. A few of them walked over to him, while another crouched on all fours behind him. Then, before he knew what was happening, they pushed him over. When he fell down, they sat on his arms and legs, and one pulled down his pants.

"Over there women raped ten-year-old boys," explained Rosenberg. "The men marched off to war as if into water. They never came back."

The milkmaid had a sixteen-year-old daughter. One evening Rosenberg came home and saw that all his things had been moved to the daughter's room. He waited until her mother returned and asked

what it meant. She called her daughter. "What's this all about?" And
the daughter answered, *"Khvatit, mamasha, tepyer ya!" That's enough for
you, Mama, my turn now!*

The comrades on the Polish party's Central Committee, whom
Uszer and Rosenberg had known in Wronki, had been interrogated
in the Kremlin. They were ordered to admit to treason. The leaders
of the Polish party were indignant. "Are you the only ones who know
what's right?" they asked. "How can you be so sure? And how can we
be sure you're right? After all, you're no saints and communism is
rationalism, not idolatry!" That's how they'd answer. Even beating
didn't help. So another approach was tried. They were told candidly
that the accusations brought against them were now known by the
entire working class and couldn't be retracted. The party couldn't per-
mit itself to admit it made mistakes. That's just what their enemies
were waiting for! The party could especially not tolerate differences
to exist in the Communist movement, differences that could result in
a schism and do great damage to the cause. As Communists, they
should be able to understand this themselves. And it was precisely of
doing, or attempting to do, such damage, consciously or unconsciously, that they, the Polish Communists, were being accused. They
were being accused by the great Bolshevik party, which was the first
to show how to acquire and exercise power, and for that reason not
only had the right but the obligation to guide all other Communist
parties. As Communists—if they were true Communists—they ought
to understand that, regardless of their private opinions on these or
other matters, their admission of guilt was now the only solution that
could be useful to the cause. It would serve as a warning to others,
and as a medicine for their discipline, vigilance, strength. This was
the final, and in the present situation the only, service that they, as
experienced Communists, could still render their party, the working
class, and its cause.

"And they admitted it?"

"Yes. For the good of the cause. And when they were being executed, they shouted 'Long live the revolution! Long live communism!
Long live the party!'"

"What crap!" exclaimed Uszer. "Disgusting! You couldn't imagine
anything worse!"

"What do you know? What do you know about Russia?" said Rosenberg, staring at his glass. "Imagine your whole life in a concentration camp, not just three years. And what's more, nobody wants you to die. On the contrary, they want you to live! And as long as possible. Isn't that worse than Mauthausen?"

"No," said Uszer. "Life, no matter how bad, is still life. But why don't they protest? Why don't they complain! . . ."

"A Russian doesn't complain. You don't know the Russian character."

"They're afraid! Or else they don't know any other life."

"They're not afraid. The Russians aren't afraid of anything. And they're well aware there's another kind of life. They're just ashamed to admit how bad off they are. They see there's nothing they can do about it. They don't see any way out. And they've got to live. . . . A man lives as best he can. That holds true everywhere. And nowhere more than in Russia."

"What did they say about what the Germans did to the Jews?"

"In Russia they only speak about the 'crimes of the enemy against the peoples of occupied countries.'"

"But what about the murder of their own Jews? What about Kiev, Odessa?"

"They said the Soviet people suffered, and they called for vengeance on the enemy. From an internationalist point of view, it makes no difference anyway."

"If it makes no difference, then why not say what happened?"

"The reasons are not clear yet, but the party always knows what it's doing."

"Here, the party needs the Jews. They haven't got anyone else they can depend on. On the other hand, unofficially they're helping Jews emigrate to Palestine. To spite England, of course. And to get some influence there. A question of tactics! . . . Young people are leaving. After everything that's happened, they want to be, as they say, in their own place. You can't blame them. They don't trust anyone anymore. But what are older people like us supposed to do? After going through hell, leave for Palestine? And deal with Englishmen, and with Arabs? And what then? Eat stones? . . . Here, after the pogrom in Kielce, the party became the defender of the Jews. But, on the other hand, nobody was punished for the pogrom. They're conducting a shrewd policy here. Still, the best thing is to leave. Of course, if you've got somewhere to go."

"Sure, if you've got somewhere to go. And some kind of skill, too," said Rosenberg thoughtfully.

Uszer didn't tell Rosenberg that we were leaving for Venezuela soon. You didn't tell such things, even to your best friend.

A week later, Rosenberg came to see Uszer with a business proposition.

"You're in business?" Uszer asked in surprise.

"And you're not?" replied Rosenberg.

The deal concerned a truckful of one hundred percent pure wool, the likes of which hadn't been available for a long time. Not just one truck, two of them! And a third if need be. And to top it off, dirt cheap.

"How much is 'dirt cheap'?" asked Uszer.

"How much! The money doesn't matter."

"The money doesn't matter! Then what does?"

"Don't you understand? The man is leaving. Tomorrow, the day after. He'll pack his bags and be gone. He has to. . . ."

"Is this legal?"

"Legal, illegal! What's legal in this country anyway? The stuff isn't stolen, and you'll get all the papers. Well, how about it?"

"I've got to think it over."

"If you think too long, somebody else will take it, and neither of us will make anything off it. Believe me, I wouldn't come to anyone else with this deal. You and I go way back."

Uszer, Nusen, and Fryd went to have a look at the merchandise, and they liked it very much. They could make a good, fast profit on it. They wouldn't have to scrounge around anymore. A chance like this, just as they were leaving, was a gift from heaven. But the wool had to be paid for in dollars, large bills. No tens, twenties, or even fifties. They wouldn't even take hundreds, only five-hundred-dollar bills, known as "barrels."

The goods would cost two barrels, maybe three. A barrel cost more than five hundred dollars in smaller banknotes, and they weren't easy to obtain. But in this case you could double your money, and, with a thousand dollars in your pocket, you had something to face the world with. What's more, the risk wasn't great. Uszer knew Rosenberg from before the war; they'd been in prison together.

Nusen and Fryd decided to chip in a barrel each. The Meinemers were the only ones who didn't go in. They had their papers for Belgium already, were packed, and were no longer doing any business. They were waiting to sell a house of theirs in Rembertów, for which they already had a buyer.

My mother went to Pabianice and Ozorków and brought back three barrels. Nusen got hold of an army truck, and Fryd made a deal with the janitor for the use of an additional cellar.

Uszer handed over the money for the goods to Rosenberg. Rosenberg hadn't wanted to take the money himself. He said that, since it wasn't for him, Uszer should go with him and pay the owner himself. Uszer didn't agree. He said he'd only give the dollars to Rosenberg, and only in private, because he didn't trust anybody else. Rosenberg had to agree.

They brought the wool to the courtyard and unloaded it casually in broad daylight, just as if it were an ordinary delivery. The driver and the janitor helped out. After the truck had made its second trip back and the last of the wool had been unloaded, a jeep drove up into the courtyard, and four civilians in high boots got out.

My mother was just returning from the store with her groceries. She walked up the stairs and saw the seal of the Special Commission on our door. The bag of groceries fell from her hands. Regaining her composure, she turned back, but slipped on spilled sour cream, fell, and cut her forehead. Not realizing blood was trickling down her face, she ran to the people who had moved into the Gaworczyks' place, to ask them to open the door that lead from their side of the apartment to ours, of which the Special Commission was apparently unaware. But the neighbors were terrified by the way my mother looked and wouldn't even hear of opening the door for her.

"Then why don't you leave the house and I'll open it myself!" urged my mother. "You can say you knew nothing about it! . . . I beg you, let me do it! My child and I are being left out on the street. If I don't get in there now, we'll have nothing to live on, nothing to wear. . . . In the name of your own children, I beg you!"

They agreed to leave the apartment. My mother pushed aside a large barrel in which our neighbors kept water. The barrel was full, and my mother had to move it all by herself. She didn't have the key to the door, so she broke the lock. Then, with a strength she hadn't suspected she had, she pushed back the wardrobe standing on our side of the door. Again she stumbled, cutting her mouth this time. Holding her mouth with one hand to leave no traces of blood, she took a fifty-dollar bill hidden in the linen and a four-yard length of silk. She tossed some clothes and warm underwear into a suitcase, threw on her prewar overcoat, which Mrs. Dziurewicz had given back to her in Mińsk Mazowiecki, and closed the wardrobe. On her way out, she looked through the window and saw Uszer being escorted across the courtyard. She pulled the wardrobe back, closed the door behind her, and put the water barrel back where it had been before.

Escorted into the apartment, Uszer saw that the wardrobe wasn't in place and knew that my mother had been there, which reassured him. He said he didn't know anything about any dollars and had never had any. He was borne out by a thorough search in which nothing was found.

Uszer took the same position during the interrogation.

"And what about these?" said the investigator, sticking two barrels under his nose. "You don't recognize them?"

"No," said Uszer, examining the five-hundred-dollar bills with amazement. For some reason the third barrel was missing. "Where would I get that kind of money?"

The investigator gestured to a man in high boots standing by the door. The door was opened and in walked Rosenberg. He was also wearing high boots.

The lawyer told Uszer to take the entire blame. He advised Uszer to say he had bought the goods and paid for them, not with dollars, but with regular Polish currency, part of which he had borrowed from Nusen and Fryd. Nusen and Fryd, as the principal owners of the stand, were only supposed to sell the goods at a reasonable profit. Uszer was neither a speculator nor a black marketeer dealing in foreign currencies. He bought legal merchandise. Rosenberg, who had persuaded him to buy it, had guaranteed him that it was legal, and

Uszer had intended to sell it legally. The business with the dollars was just a trick, a slander, a plot.

In this manner, the lawyer saved Nusen and Fryd and succeeded in getting them released on bail. In the lawyer's opinion, even with the best defense, Uszer's conviction was inevitable. But he hoped that, in view of Uszer's prewar Communist activities and his imprisonment for them as well as his years in the Nazi concentration camps, the sentence wouldn't be stiff.

Meanwhile my mother and I were without a roof over our heads. We'd spend the nights with the Nusens and Fryds. The Meinemers left soon after Uszer, Nusen, and Fryd were arrested. They didn't even wait to sell the house they had inherited in Rembertów. A Jewish family who had come back from Russia was now living in their room. Izak Fryd had already been sent abroad with a kibbutz of Shomer Hatzair.

As soon as Nusen and Fryd were released, their wives, both of them with infants—there was no problem of circumcision since both children were girls—packed a suitcase each and left to "take the waters" in Krynica. When they had safely crossed the border, Nusen and Fryd took a cab to the train station, carrying no suitcases, only a briefcase each.

From then on we slept at our neighbors' and with other people we knew. We went from one to the other, staying two or three nights. We didn't stay any longer than that because their apartments were crowded as it was and we couldn't be bothering them. It was kind of them to let us spend even a night. No one, not even a completely innocent person, wanted anything to do with the UB or the Special Commission.

People who were arrested by the Special Commission had their apartments sealed; if they were found guilty, the apartment, their furniture, and any other goods of value were confiscated. And the times were gone when you could give a soldier a thousand zlotys and get yourself another apartment. All the apartments had long since been taken, even the attics and basements. And no new buildings had been built.

My mother, however, didn't give up. She ran to every last government office. She told them what we had been through during the Occupation. She wept. But that didn't do any good now. The officials shrugged. In a case like this they couldn't do anything for her. They advised her to try in Warsaw.

My mother went to Warsaw. But in Warsaw they wouldn't even talk to her. She wasn't even allowed into the building.

It was winter, snow was falling. My mother stood in front of the building and peered at the people entering and leaving. She stood there until nightfall. Suddenly a car pulled up and stopped in front of the main entrance. An older man came out of the building. When my mother saw him getting into the car, she ran over and grabbed the door. It was the same man who had given us the apartment allocation in Łódź.

"Comrade Jasinski!" cried my mother. "Don't you recognize me? I'm the woman who survived the war with her child on Aryan papers! Try and remember me! I've come from Łódź! You've got to help me! Remember, you gave me an allocation for an apartment?"

The chauffeur was about to push my mother away from the car.

"One moment!" Jasinski stopped him. "Yes, I remember you. What's the matter? What's happened?"

"I don't have the apartment anymore! They took it away! It's winter and they've put me and my child on the streets!"

"But who's done this, and why?"

"I don't know why. It's just plain human baseness! I beg you, help me, I'm all alone in the world, only you can help me!"

"Don't cry. . . . Come tomorrow at nine o'clock. We'll see what can be done."

My mother didn't come at nine; she was there at eight. But the doorkeeper wouldn't let her in, and so she waited outside. There was a heavy frost that day. My mother couldn't stand still and kept walking back and forth to stay warm. At nine o'clock she knocked again.

"You again?" asked the doorkeeper through a grate-covered opening in the door.

"I've already told you I have an appointment with Comrade Jasinski."

"Comrade Jasinski isn't receiving anyone," said the doorkeeper.

"But I have an appointment with him! Ask him, he'll tell you. . . ."

"Don't tell me what to do!" said the doorkeeper, then closed the opening and walked away.

My mother didn't leave the door. An hour later a mailman came. Seeing it was the mailman, the doorkeeper opened the door. My mother raced in behind the mailman. The doorkeeper grabbed her and tried to push her out. My mother started crying. A door to an office opened, and Comrade Jasinski appeared in the door.

My mother told him the whole truth. She didn't even conceal the part about the dollars. She said that her husband had fallen prey to a planned provocation, one especially disgusting since it had originated from a former colleague in the party, a man with whom Uszer had once been imprisoned in the same cell. For being Communists. Of his forty years, her husband had spent four in Wronki prison, two in the Warsaw ghetto, and three in a concentration camp. He had been through the selection in Treblinka, survived Mauthausen. Wasn't that enough for one man? Why did he have to go to prison again, now, when he had come back to life again? Had he done anyone any harm? Did he have any criminal intentions? It was just provocation! Do you go to a man and persuade him to do something illegal just so you can put him in prison? That's simply beyond comprehension. Even the Germans didn't do things like that! What was really going on here? Informing on someone, that you understand, that's nothing new. But to come and provoke someone so you can have something to inform on him with? And to do it to an old friend? And so his wife and child are left freezing in the streets? And for this a person is rewarded with a job? Is this how people work their way up these days? Are these sorts of people going to be given official positions now? Then no one can feel secure anymore. Is this why we survived the war? That man didn't see any real war. If he'd been through what we had, he wouldn't have done it. But over there, in Russia, all they taught him was provocation and denunciation. Who needs it? And for what? Aren't there enough real criminals? Aren't there enough people in prisons? Can't a court understand such simple things?

"I believe you. Unfortunately, things like that are happening now," said Jasinski. "But will the court believe it? . . . The court knows only one thing: a crime has been committed. This is a very tough case, not much can be done. The only thing I can do is to try and get you your apartment back." Jasinski picked up the receiver and, with my mother still there, called Łódź.

My mother boarded a train and was at the Special Commission in
Łódź by four o'clock.

"So you went to Warsaw to complain about us," said the official to
whom my mother reported for the key.

"I'll go again if I have to," replied my mother.

"Well, watch out you don't go too far. . . ."

"Don't try to scare me. I've been up against worse than you . . . ,"
said my mother. "Just give me the key!"

With the key clasped tightly in her hand, my mother staggered
up the stairs. She tore off the seal and opened the door. Holding onto
the wall, she walked to the bed and collapsed on it.

My mother stayed in bed two weeks. She had pneumonia. But, if she
hadn't gotten in to see Jasinski, our apartment, along with our furniture and other things, would have been given to Rosenberg. A ruling
to that effect had already been signed.

People brought us food and could not contain their admiration for
my mother. "You've worked a miracle," they said. "To get an apartment back from them, that takes know-how! No wonder you got
through the war."

We did get the apartment back, but there wasn't a cent left of the
fifty dollars my mother had managed to retrieve from the wardrobe.
We didn't have any money to pay Uszer's lawyer or to live on. So,
as soon as my mother was well again, she went to Mińsk Mazowiecki
to see Janczewski, a notary public who had lived in Dobre before
the war.

Janczewski hired a car and drove to Dobre with my mother in order to sell the fourth part of the apartment building we'd inherited
from my grandfather. They didn't go see anyone in Dobre. They just
pulled up in front of the inn where they had an appointment with
the person who wanted to buy our fourth of the building.

The man they were supposed to meet was late, so they ordered
lunch. Suddenly a dirty, unshaven peasant came into the inn. He ordered a vodka, drank it down, then, lolling in his chair, looked at my
mother with that ugly smile men like him use when looking at Jews.

"Tell her," he said, addressing all those present, "she'd better clear
out of here if she doesn't want to be shorter by a head!"

My mother's spoon fell from her hand. Janczewski the notary stood up, took my mother by the arm, and led her from the inn at once. They got into the car and drove off.

"It's not enough for them!" Mr. Janczewski said. "They haven't lined their pockets enough yet. . . . Don't come back here again! They're capable of anything. . . . Don't come back here again, I beg you."

The lawyer took no money for defending Uszer. He had gotten a retainer for defending Nusen and Fryd, but, since they had fled and he didn't have to defend them, he said he would require no further payment, not even for making the appeal. Uszer had originally been sentenced to five years in prison with the possibility of being transferred to a labor camp, where, depending on his productivity, each day could count as a day and a half. The lawyer filed an appeal and obtained a reduction in the sentence to four years from the time of arrest.

My mother wanted to place me back in Helenówek. She applied to the Jewish Committee, but all she got was two containers of cocoa and some winter clothing. Mrs. Rotholz wouldn't accept me back. "There's no place for the children of speculators in our Children's Home," she said.

However, there were people on the Jewish Committee who had a sense of my mother's predicament. They directed me to take a medical examination. I was lucky—it turned out there actually was something wrong with my lungs, and I was sent to a sanatorium for children, far from Łódź, in the Sudeten Mountains.

Again we wore American clothes and swallowed American vitamins. We found German sleds, skis, and postage stamps in the attic. Whole boxes of stamps with Hitler's face on them. We'd bring these boxes down from the attic, set them down in the middle of the room, then grab handfuls of stamps and throw them up in the air like confetti. Once again we believed we had won the war.

In the morning, a nurse jingling with thermometers would wake us up. If you had no fever, you put on skis and went to school. In school we were asked about our "persuasion." Those who didn't understand the question answered, "From the sanatorium." They were marked down as "Judaic." The older boys said, "None!" in protest.

The teacher would smile, say, "None? Impossible," and write down "Judaic."

We liked our teacher, although he spared us no beatings for disobedience. We all studied in one room, the third, fourth, and fifth grades together, not because there were too few rooms but because there weren't enough teachers. We were behind in our schooling. The boys in the fifth grade were taller than the teacher, and they laughed when he hit them with a wooden ruler on their hands or behinds. When he asked if that was enough, they'd answer, "No!" and take more. We, the smaller boys, followed their example and like them shouted, "No!" although it really hurt us. We liked the teacher because he beat us without malice, creating the sort of intimate relationship for which we unconsciously longed—few of us could remember our fathers. So, in the morning, if the mercury was too high, we'd stealthily shake the thermometer under the covers so they would let us go to school.

We were irradiated with artificial light, and we lounged in deck chairs on the verandas, taking the open air while our teachers read us stories from the novel *The Heart* by the Italian writer Edmondo de Amicis. In the evenings they'd tell us about the English, American, and Russian films they'd made special trips to see in a town almost twenty miles away. Both in the books they read us and in the movies they told us about the good people always won out. Even if they lost their lives. We listened intently, dying and triumphing along with the heroes.

Our teachers were grownups and had lived through the war as grownups. It could not be said they were deceiving us. At that time they still did not know how slight the difference is between peace and war, war that never really ends but only hides beneath the surface of life and continues its course there. People feel this and that is why they are constantly afraid of something. In a certain way real war may be better: during a war you can wait for peace. And truly believe in it.

Our teachers wanted to make us believe in the victory. And in that they succeeded. You can't hold a grudge against them for that. But a grudge can be held against others. Our teachers believed in the victory because they were grownups and thought that, once people had committed a great error, they'd know how to prevent it from happening again. And we believed in the victory because we were children.

We thought that a war like the one we'd lived through happens only once in a lifetime; if you survived, you were completely safe. And we had the war behind us.

One thing brought me up short. Uszer was in prison. Alone again, my mother was running around a strange city, with pieces of illegal fabric in her suitcase, bribing guards to send Uszer packages in prison. And my father was in his grave. Near Radoszyna. By the road. The grass grew taller there and had a distinctly different color. Every day people passed by it on their way back and forth to the fields. And no one had had the courage to say who had killed him. No one had even had the courage to ask. . . .

So how did the war really end?

❁

Afterword to *The Victory*

I was in Moscow in August 1991 in the heady days after the coup had failed and Russia felt like a free country. Speaking of the three young men killed by the putschists, a Russian friend said to me, "One of those young men was a Jew. And, now that Jewish blood has been shed for Russia's freedom, there can never be any question of any anti-Semitism in this country ever again!" I did not say it—that statement is a measure of exaltation and not of objective reality. I did not say anything. I do remember thinking, if fleetingly, of *The Victory* at that moment.

The tragic tidings this book bears are that we do not learn from our mistakes and never change. Anti-Semitism did not disappear in Poland after the Holocaust any more than it would in Russia after a young Jew had died for Russia's freedom. Not only evil in general but particular evils abide.

But this quiet and harrowing book should not in the least be taken as anything like an indictment of Polish anti-Semitism, a subject on which there is considerable confusion. The Polish fascists were strong in the late thirties—anti-Semitic propaganda was rife, Jews were beaten in the streets. During the Nazi Occupation, some Poles were indifferent to the slaughter of the Jews, some derived that malicious pleasure for which only the Germans have a word, *Schadenfreude*, and some simply profited by taking over the victims' furniture, jewels, apartments, and stores. There were of course "righteous" Poles who saved the lives of Jews at the risk of their own. But even the anti-Semites took no real hand in the crime. Grynberg himself in an essay entitled "Altera Pars" says, "Polish anti-Semitism did not have a ho-micidal aspect. It was never any nastier than Russian, French, Hungarian or Argentinian anti-Semitism." And this is a statement made by a person who, in 1968, appalled by the resurgence of anti-Semitism used for political ends in Communist Poland, chose to remain in America while on tour with Ida Kaminska's Yiddish Theatre and has lived here since.

Grynberg, who was born in Warsaw in 1936, essentially describes his own fate and that of his family in this book, which is autobiography and history told as fiction. In fact, it is part of a series of similar painful, plainspoken novellas. The first, *The Jewish War*, chronicles the narrator's life during the Occupation, while the later works deal with his youth in Communist Poland and the particular perils of his profession. As he says, "I became a writer of the dead—the living have enough writers of their own." The period covered in *The Victory* is 1944 to 1947, that is, from the final months of the Second World War to the final stages of the Communist takeover.

This is a complex and painful passage in Poland's history. Between the wars, the country had enjoyed a brief interlude of independence and sovereignty after having disappeared from the map of Europe for over a century. In the opening pages of *The Victory* we see Poland as it emerges from the Nazi Occupation and the Holocaust. It is no longer a society but has become a jungle of Darwinian ferocity. The struggle for existence and the struggle for power are constant. And the two are related—people with power do not die of hunger.

To some extent, the struggle for political power had an absurdist element. As became clear soon enough, Stalin had taken the eastern half of Europe as his booty. This had been agreed upon at Yalta and was never seriously questioned by the West in all the years that followed until the miraculous demise of communism in Eastern Europe and in Russia itself.

But that wasn't clear in the heat of the moment. Some Poles believed in fighting all enemies to the end; a few may even have believed they were making more than another of the doomed and gallant gestures that mark much of Polish history, while others may have hoped that resistance could produce concessions from the new rulers. When the war ended, the Narodówka (nickname for the NSZ, a right-wing organization) simply switched from killing Germans to killing Communists and Jews, which were, in their minds, one and the same. At times, the activities of this and other "partisan" groups were indistinguishable from banditry and marauding. The Home Army, known as the AK, was a respectable nationalist partisan fighting group that took part in the Warsaw Uprising of 1944. It is fitting that Big Władek, the just and honest policeman in this story, should have served with the AK during the war. The soldiers of the Red Army marching endlessly from the east are also treated sympathetically here. The danger is from the NKVD, as the KGB was known then, an organization that changed its initials often but its nature never. They were in Poland to continue the job they had begun when in the early days of the war they had, on Stalin's orders, massacred fifteen thousand Polish officers—the country's elite who could not be allowed to return to Poland after the war and form the nucleus of a society unfriendly to the Soviet Union.

Though there are killings and betrayals in this story, it is not the dramas that are most shocking but the behavior of people in daily life. With the ashes of an immense tragedy still in the air, people bicker over coats and sewing machines. And there could be nothing quite as painful as the recriminations of two Jewish mothers who have both lost children. This sorrowful story creates a special irony of its own, which suffuses the work from its very title to its very last line. Here irony is not a literary device, a way of achieving psychological distance; it is the dynamic between what should have been and what was not. Shortly after the end of the war there was a pogrom in the Polish town of Kielce. Nothing had been learned, no value derived. The enemy is defeated, the peace signed. But the war has not ended. The war never ends.

RICHARD LOURIE
SEPTEMBER 1, 1993

✿

About the Author

Henryk Grynberg, born in 1936 in Warsaw, Poland, survived the Holocaust in hiding and on so-called Aryan papers. He is the author of twenty-four books of prose, poetry, essays, and drama, and his work has been translated into English, French, German, Italian, Dutch, Hebrew, and Czech. Grynberg, who lives in Virginia, has received many literary awards, including the Jan Karski and Pola Nirenska award. His *Children of Zion* was published by Northwestern University Press in 1997.

❖

Jewish Lives

INGEBORG HECHT
Invisible Walls *and* To Remember Is to Heal

DAN JACOBSON
Heshel's Kingdom

SZYMON LAKS
Music of Another World

ERICH LEYENS AND LOTTE ANDOR
Years of Estrangement

RUTH LIEPMAN
Maybe Luck Isn't Just Chance

ERIC LUCAS
The Sovereigns: A Jewish Family in the German Countryside

ARNOŠT LUSTIG
The Bitter Smell of Almonds
Children of the Holocaust
The House of Returned Echoes
The Unloved (From the Diary of Perla S.)

LIANNA MILLU
Smoke over Birkenau

ZOFIA NAŁKOWSKA
Medallions

BERNHARD PRESS
The Murder of the Jews in Latvia, 1941–1945

ARMIN SCHMID AND RENATE SCHMID
Lost in a Labyrinth of Red Tape

WIKTORIA ŚLIWOWSKA, ED.
The Last Eyewitnesses: Children of the Holocaust Speak